Cherished by a Boss

A.J. Davidson

Cherished by a Boss

Copyright © 2017 by A.J. Davidson

Published by Mz. Lady P Presents

www.mzladypresents.com

Dedication:

This book is dedicated to my boys Jarrett and Ashton. Mommy is trying so hard to make you two proud of her. You would think it would be the other way around. Everything I do is to show you guys that you can do anything you put your mind to. Never let anyone tell you what you cannot do. That is one thing you will never hear mommy say. Regardless of where you go in life, just know I am always in your corner rooting for you and pushing you to beat the odds. I love you both with every fiber in my bones, even though they are aching right now as I type this. Lol, I love you babies. Muahhhh xoxo Mommy

Acknowledgments

BOOK 3, WOW!!!

This is still really hard to believe. Little ole country/proper Ashley from Columbus, MS is an author now. First, I would like to thank God because without this gifted mind that he gave me I would not be able to hear my characters. Lol! That is a gift and a curse at the same time. Especially, when they start talking to you in your sleep, and you have to get up and write that part down or make a mental note to do it first thing in the morning.

Secondly, to my family who has been a very big support system for me. My husband for putting up with me and my typing nonstop all day long or talking about characters that he knows nothing about. But, he still sat there and listened to the story. My sisters Alicia and Asia; that Asia will make sure she gets my book as soon as it comes out and I love her so much for that. My baby brother Kayin, I love you baby boy, witcho fat self lol. My cousin British; who one of my characters is based off. She is a real firecracker, but I love her to death. We may have our ups and downs, but I promise you that girl will not let nobody mess with her Ashley.

Mama, I thank you for always saying I CAN DO IT. You wanted to purchase a book just so you could take it to work and brag on your daughter. Lol, I gotta make sure I get you that book.

Daddy, I'm doing all I can to make you proud of me. I also have a mental note in my head from you, "NO FREE BOOKS". He says I worked too hard to give books away for free. Know your worth baby girl, and I promise you it's not free.

My last book was dedicated to my grandmothers. My great grandmother passed away a few weeks after my second book was released. Before I left her house, she said how proud of me she was, and she wished me luck with my books. And for that, I will keep on pushing for you Mama Ida, Rest In Heaven I LOVE YOU! Even on the days I feel like giving up, I will keep going making sure I never let you down.

To My Readers

I cannot thank you guys enough. Whether you shared a post, purchased a paperback or eBooks, I want to say thank you thank you a million times. Without you guys, I would not be at book 3. Once you finish a book, you come right to my wall and ask WHEN IS THE NEXT ONE COMING, and that alone pushes me to keep going. Thank you. Now I know I have a lot of readers, but I have to shout out the few that I know are gone ask for an invoice for the next book before it is available. Bianca Johnson, Kierra Weaver, Ashley Justice, Avesha Fenton, Cebrone Herrod, Lauren Cole. Natalie Parker Louis (cousin), Ashley Lockett, Victoria Williams, Robert Williams, Ciera Gavin, Johnie Thomas, Ebony Blount, Taketa Ingram, Nanniah Whittle. Special acknowledgment to Chase Williams, Miguel Valentin, and my FAVORITE COUSIN British Jackson, for allowing me to use them as characters.

To My Dope Pen Sisters

Trenae', Manda P, and Latoya Nicole, you three ladies have pushed me to get this book completed. It has been plenty, and I do mean plenty, of times where I wanted to give up, but you guys pushed me and challenged me to get it completed. If you haven't read any of their books, you better get them because you are truly missing out on a good read.

Oh, trust me I can't forget about my entire MLPP team. Let's keep grinding and pushing out these dope books. We are under the hottest publisher out, so there's no excuse for us to fail when she is giving us all the tools we need to succeed.

My Super Awesome Bad Azz Publisher

I can't forget the DOPEST publisher of them all, MZLADYP!!!I love the fact that she can go into teacher mode real quick and teach you what you need to know to make yourself better as an author, to make your brand stand out, and to make your books bomb. She wants you to succeed, so she makes sure she gives you the real. I swear I love her for that. Keep up the great work! You are amazing! Thanks for taking me under your wing!!

KEEP UP WITH A.J

Facebook: Author AJ Davidson
Like Page: Author AJ Davidson
Readers Group: AJ Tha Pen Pusha:
Instagram:Aj_penpusha
Twitter: aj_penpusha

Table of Contents

Chapter 1

London "Cookie" Bridges

It became a routine for me to sit in my driveway once I pulled up at home. The thought of walking in the house to a man that you have completely fallen out of love with has always made my skin crawl. It was not always like this, at one point we were happy. Dangerously in love is how I like to think of it. Brandon was once the love of my life. But, you know how you have that gut feeling that your man is cheating on you. Some call it "a woman's intuition" and the majority of the time, you're right.

He starts slowly changing into this other person— the one who always starts arguments to leave the house, and the one who always accuses you because he is really the one out there doing wrong. The canceled dinner dates, the forgetful anniversary days. Brandon became that guy! The guy who I loved to hate.

I already know when I get out of this car, as soon as I open the door there will be words coming at me like a boomerang. Any little thing I said wrong, he would blow up on me. If he is not arguing, he just sits there and ignores the shit out of me. You would think because I have it all together, career wise that he would be pleased with that, but regardless of what I do, it's never enough for him.

Just to tell you a little bit about me, I'm London Bridges, but people call me Cookie. I am 27 years old— 28 on July 9th. Team Cancer baby!

Currently, I am an elementary school teacher going into my third year of teaching. I'm 5'7, honey brown skin tone, I have the body females would pay to have. Seriously, it looks like I have had more surgeries than the Kardashians. My hair is long, and I like to wear it bone straight, even though it's naturally curly.

Now Brandon, my gosh, that man still gives me butterflies when he walks into the room. But then he opens his mouth and speaks to me, and those butterflies fly away quickly. He would be the perfect guy if God would have made him with no tongue, so he would not be so damn disrespectful. You know the bad thing about B is, he knows he is fine and that a lot of women in our little town want him. Hell, even old ass grandmas like to throw themselves at him, not giving 2 fucks if I am right there with him, and I have had just about enough of it.

Finally, I started to get out of my car, dreading walking into this house. I reached behind my seat, grabbed my test papers, and headed in.

"Hello," I said as soon as I laid eyes on him. He was standing in the mirror adjusting his tie.

"Hello," I spoke again and still no words. We have not said one word to each other since I left for work this morning, and he does not even look like he is happy to see me.

"I take it that you are headed out to a meeting?" I asked as I threw my Jessica Simpson heels to the side of the bed.

"Yes!" he replied as he sprayed on that Kenneth Cole Black cologne I bought him, that instantly made my pussy wet when I smelled it.

I really can't do anything but shake my head at him. As much as I want to think he is actually going to a meeting, I can't. No meeting last more than three hours, no meeting will make you sometimes not even come home. On the nights he does not come home, he always says, *"You know I hate leaving a deal unfinished."*

I know you guys may say I'm crazy because the signs are there, but this is my husband, my first love, my everything. When I first met him, everything about him demanded attention whenever he was in someone's presence, and I was just the person to give it to him. He wined and dined me from day one. When no one else was there for me, he made sure I had whatever I needed, making me feel like I was the only woman in the world. It was always supposed to be London and Brandon, and each morning that I woke up to him, he made each day as special as the last. So understand leaving, is not always that easy, when you have invested so much money and time into a person. I thought back to the first day my friend Noelle introduced us to each other.

3 years ago

Pulling up to Noelle's apartment, I blew my horn so she could hurry up and come outside before we missed the movie we were going to see. She ran out the door, jumped in the car, and instantly started applying lipstick.

"Hey booooo," she spoke after she finished putting on her lipstick."

"Aww hell here we go, the only time you say boo like that is when you're about to ask me to do something you know I am going to say no to. So, spill it!"

"I have no earthly idea what you are talking about."

I knew she was lying, so I just sat there a little while tapping on my stirring wheel until she started talking.

"Ok, ok, ook, so I met this guy name Matt right, and I really, really like him and want to get to know him better. He moved here from Chicago. Right now, he is staying with his cousin Brandon until he finds a place. He asked if I had a girl for his cousin." She paused for a second waiting to see if I would say something. "Soooo, that's where you come in. I want us to go on a double date. You can pretend to get to know his guy and also help me feel out Matt, and no his cousin is not ugly, he is extremely fucking fine, actually."

"Come on Noelle, you know I do not do blind dates. If this man comes out looking like Young Thug, I'ma hurt his damn feelings. Besides, I have so much going on, I have a ton of papers to grade, and the last thing I need is this stank breath man all up in my face, feeding me a bunch of lies," I replied

"Cookie, I promise you he is a great guy. On top of that, he has his own barbershop called Klean Kuts. He is fine as hell, and when I say fine, I mean panty droppa type fine. You know that last accident I hooked you up with had a few teeth missing," She started holding in her laugh. "Well, Brandon has the prettiest teeth; I *know that is a major plus in your book, oh and get this, you can even see this nigga dick print through his pants."*

"Girl shut up!" I quickly replied. "You're going into deep details. I'm starting to think you want his ass. You know I never go behind you, so if you want him don't hook me up with him. We already had this issue once," I replied, rolling my eyes at the thought of what she did.

"Why you gotta bring up old shit, London?"

I can see she was getting irritated, but I didn't give a damn. She always wants to hook me up with a man, then when I dump his ass, she goes and makes him feel all better by fucking the shit out of him.

Let me tell you a little about my best friend, Noelle. She has this pretty brown skin complexion, skinny but she swears she thick as hell. She keeps a fresh set of bundles in that head of hers. We have been friends since our 9th-grade year. If we are out in public, you always will see one of us and just know the other one is not far behind. She knows about my last relationship, how he cheated on me and the last thing I want to do is jump into another relationship. At this point, I feel all men are the same.

"Just meet him first then you can decide if you want to talk to him or not. If you think he is ugly, then I will leave back out of the restaurant with you."

"Wait, who said anything about a date? You just said you wanted me to meet him and now you're throwing in there that we are going to a restaurant," I sassed.

"Look, girl you need to get out the house anyway, it's the weekend. You can grade those papers tomorrow and get this I will even help you," she insisted.

When it comes down to men and Noelle, there isn't one she hasn't let slide up in her. Sooner or later she gone have to get her a new pussy like Sky did from Black Ink New York. Noelle and I are the complete opposites. I like to let my men chase me, and she likes to chase them. I like earning my own money, and she likes doing something strange for a little piece of their change. See, like I said we are the complete opposites.

I agreed to go on a date with them, and if things went left, I'm running out of that restaurant like I'm Speedy Gonzalez.

***

We walked into this nice ass Italian place; it was packed from corner to corner. The waitress led us to the table where the men were already seated. I looked at Brandon, and my heart started pounding, and my damn hands started sweating like I was standing in the middle of a heat wave in Arizona. I had forgotten all about having my guard up. At this point, I'm like, what broken heart? He was fine as hell; he had that Super Cali Swagilistic Sexy Hella Dopeness, thing going on. Brandon had me grinning like a high school girl when her crush spoke to her for the first time. I swear I was showing all 32 teeth, my smile stretched from ear to ear when he stood up and pulled my seat out.

He was at least 6'1, 200 pounds, light brown skin, with a clean cut goatee. His eyes pulled me in. Oh my, his eyes will have you in a trance all day just looking into them— they were this hazel color, his skin was as smooth as whipped caramel, those lips looked like he could suck my whole coochie at once. We sat at that restaurant for hours just laughing and talking just really trying to get to know each other. He wasn't married, no kids, great job, own house, own teeth, and y'all know I love that shit. The last thing on my mind was running out of that restaurant, but today, I wish I would have.

"What time will you be home? I wanted to cook us a nice dinner so we can enjoy each other for once."

"I'm not sure. It depends on how good the meeting is going. It may carry me into the next day. You know I'm all about closing the deal. I'm trying to open another shop with a new partner this time, and we have to make sure we are on the same page and shit."

If only I could knock his ass over the head and make him look at me, I want him to look at me and see how beautiful I am. Look at me how he used to look at me. He used to look at me like I was the only woman on the planet for him. But now, he just looks at me! There's nothing special about it; I'm just his wife. Apparently, that doesn't mean anything to anyone but myself.

"Ok, well maybe I will call up Noelle and see if she wants to go out and have drinks or something," I added.

"Give Noelle a break, she just got into town, plus, you two are always getting into something together. Those ways of hers are starting to rub off on you. Why don't you call up another one of your friends, one of the friends who are not sleeping with every man under the sun? I will even pay for everything just make sure you have a nice ass time, let your hair down and enjoy life for once. You are always stuck in this house grading papers and making lesson plans."

Now, this is something totally new. He has never just volunteered for me to get out the house. He is usually happy when I'm in the house, which is how it is every weekend, due to the meetings he has every Friday at seven o'clock sharp.

"Yea, you're right, I will call up British to see what her plans are for tonight. She's always down for a free meal and drinks." He gave me a peck on the forehead and quickly made an exit out of the house.

I sent British a quick text to see what she was doing tonight. She is always the best person to get my mind off things.

Me: Hey, cousin. If you're free tonight, let's have drinks.

B: Bitch, now you know I'm always down for drinks, just tell me what time I need to meet you.

Me: Mi Hacienda at 7?

B: I will be there at 6:55 waiting with bells on.

Me: LOL, bitch bye.

That damn British is always saying something crazy.

It's six o'clock now, so I have a little time to get dressed. *It's not like I'm going out to meet someone, so sweats and a t-shirt and my hair in a bun will be good enough for drinks,* I thought to myself.

The vibration from my cell phone pulled my attention.

B: DO NOT PUT ON NO DAMN SWEATS. BITCH, I KNOW YO ASS.

Me: Those were not my intentions at all; I have a cute little outfit in mind.

B: The lies you tell. Put them damn sweat pants up, London Bridges.

Shit, now she knows I like to be comfortable when I'm going to engage in adult activities.

Walking into my closet, I tried to piece together the cutest little outfit I could find. I found my distressed skinny leg jeans that made my ass look extra juicy, an off the shoulder shirt that was loose fitting, with a pair of stilettos.

Looking at the time it was 6:45, so I grabbed my Coach purse and headed out the door. I jumped into my 2016 all black Lexus and sped off to the restaurant.

Getting out of my car, I adjusted my tits in this uncomfortable ass bra and walked into the building. My eyes locked with this fine ass man sitting at the bar as I looked around for my cousin. The look on his face had me literally standing there in a daze. I'm not sure how long I was looking until I felt British tug on my arm.

"Girl come on, I've been sitting over there waving at yo ass so you could see me, and you're just standing there staring off into space or some shit!" she barked, pulling me into the direction of our booth.

As soon as we sat down, the waitress walked up. She was a short Spanish lady with really long hair, and her eyebrows were drawn on with precision. I mean this hoe dotted every I and crossed every T when she did those damn brows.

"Hello, I'm Josaline; I will be your waitress for tonight. Can I start you off with a drink from our happy hour special?"

"Sure! Give me the two for one peach frozen margarita with a double shot of Patron, and make the second one mango. Oh and bring them out at the same time," I spoke up and said, catching the look on British face as I finished ordering.

"Shiiiid, just give me what she's having, sound like that shit's gone be lit for real." The waitress walked off to put our orders in.

"So what's going on with you, Cookie? Usually, when we come here, you get some watered down ass drink and your usual of chicken over rice, drowned in that damn goat cheese to eat, then you're ready to run yo ass home. What's up?" she questioned.

I had to be honest. I'm really worried about my marriage. Three years of loving the same man, making love to the same man, dreaming of being with the same man years from now, and suddenly it all fades away.

My heart is broken, and the only person I want to fix it is the one that broke it. He promised me forever, and it seems like he is really ready to give it all up. I was always told to fight for my marriage, and that's what I'm going to do. The bullshit ass arguments he makes up, I will try to avoid. The name calling has to stop, and the occasional criticism must end tonight.

"Helllllo, earth to Cookie!" British snapped, pulling me from my thoughts. "You're over there tripping for real. You may not need those drinks if you are already acting like that.

"I'm good, sorry, I was just thinking about something."

"I'm listening!" she replied quickly.

"It's Brandon; I think he is having an affair."

"Hol' the fuck up! What you mean, you think he's having an affair? In order for you to think that you have to have some type of clue that gives that shit away. Text messages, hickeys, lipstick on his collar, his dick smelled like pussy, but it wasn't your pussy."

"Girl, you stupid… shut up," I said, laughing at her crazy ass. "But for real, it's the late nights coming home, we rarely have sex, and when we do, he beats my shit up like he's angry at something."

"Oh, cause I was about to say, now beating it up isn't a bad thing." She laughed, sticking her tongue out and twerking in her seat. She is a whole character for real. I can't do anything but shake my head at her.

"No bitch, it's bad when he make yo ass bleed afterwards. That nigga beats it up so hard he be slinging all my coochie juices out and be having my shit dryer than the Sahara Desert." I chuckled, causing her to burst into laughter catching the attention of others and one person in particular— the guy from the bar who I locked eyes with earlier.

"Here are your drinks," the waitress announced. "Let me know if you need anything else, enjoy!" she finished as she turned to walk away.

I grabbed my first drink and sucked it down so fast the damn room started spinning. I wanted to drown my sorrow into my drinks, the best way I could. I reached for my next drink until British pulled my hand back.

"Slow your roll, girl. Did you forget that you drove here?"

"I will be ok. If not, they got Uber everywhere," I replied. I took another sip of my drink and waited for my food to come out.

"You see cutie at the bar? He has been looking over here since you sat down," British whispered as if the man could hear her from across the room.

"I noticed him when I first walked in; he is kinda cute, huh!" I slowly turned my head towards his direction and gave him a little smile. I'm not sure if it's the drinks or me, but when he smiled back, my coochie started pulsating.

Stand down girl, that's not your husband, Stand down, I whispered to my coochie. You know every now, and then you have to give her a little pep talk.

"Shit Cookie, don't look, but he is coming this way," British whispered while kicking me multiple times under the table.

I started adjusting myself in my seat, I felt tipsy, but I did not want him to see that shit.

"Excuse me, I'm sorry to bother you, and usually I'm not so forward, but when you walked in, I couldn't help but notice how beautiful you are." I looked up at him, and I swear y'all I saw all the angels in heaven just flying around his head— halo style!

"Ok girl, here I come!" British said, waving to an imaginary person, just to excuse herself from the table. She winked at me on her way towards the bar. Now she knows if anyone sees me in here with this man alone, it's really going to be a war when I get home.

"Thank you!" was all I could say. He had me stuck again.

"I'm Chase," he announced while extending his hand. "Do you mind if I sit down?"

When he got close up to me, I really got a good look at him. He stood about 6'2, skin like coffee— that freshly brewed mocha caramel kind. He had a beard that looked like he used all SheaMoisture products on it to make that shit extra shiny and healthy looking. Both of his arms were covered in tattoos. Not jailhouse tattoos but those, I know my body is fine as fuck tattoos.

He wore this black button up with the first few buttons open, his sleeves were rolled up, some black slacks that you could see his baby leg sitting on his left thigh, his dick spoke to me before he even got close up to the table, and on his feet he wore some all black, red bottom loafers. The nigga looked like money was just dripped off the tip of his dick.

"Not at all, go right ahead," I replied, motioning for him to take a seat.

"And your name is?" he asked in an orotund tone. His voice was very pleasant. He spoke making sure you heard him loud and clear.

"It's London, everybody but my students calls me Cookie."

"Nice to meet you, Ms. Cookie."

"Are you from this area?"

"Yes, I was born and raised here," I replied.

"Oh ok, I'm just here on business, I will be leaving out of here in the morning. I know this place is about to close in a little while so what do you say we take a ride, just to get to know each other a little better. Seeing that you are not wearing a ring means you don't have a curfew, right?"

My mind was saying, *Bitch no, don't go. You're drunk, anything could happen*, and my pussy is saying, *Bitch, you better beat him to the car.*

"Well..." is all I could get out before I felt the vibration from my phone.

Brandon: I will be late coming in.

Me: It's fine I had too many drinks with British anyway, I will just crash at her place tonight.

Brandon: Great!!!!!

"Sure, I think I would like to get out of here."

I know what you guys are thinking, but he is only here for one night, so what could that possibly hurt?

Walking over to the bar where British was sitting, I whispered in her ear.

"I will meet you back at your place later."

The look of excitement came across her face so quickly like she was happy I was leaving with him. I don't know if I will regret it later, but as of right now I just want to enjoy the moment. My husband is definitely out enjoying his moment.

As soon as we got to his car, I looked at his license plate number and sent it over to my cousin. In case this nigga turns out to be crazy, at least they know who killed my ass.

Chapter 2

Chase Williams

I came to Columbus, MS on business. I have a guy here who wanted to introduce me to a few people so they can work with me. What I do will make them and myself more money. I like to look at it as a Companionship Service. I fly out to Miami where I live in the morning to start getting my other plans in order.

When I went out tonight, I had no intentions of picking anyone up. Meeting up with my little brother for a few drinks before our flight was all I had planned until she walked in. When she walked through those doors, it took everything in me not to approach her right then. Cookie was absolutely stunning, and her body was bad as hell. The perfect set of breasts, a flat stomach, and a fat ass. I'm never the type to just approach a woman because she gotta fat ass, but if her face is pretty as hell, her ass can be as flat as Kylie Jenner, before the surgery, as long as she knows how to throw it back in the bedroom.

At first, I felt like she was too much for me. She walked in with so much class about herself. Then I thought about what type of man I am. If she is what I want, then she is what I will get, and I did just that. Although I know I'm that nigga, that didn't stop my ass from feeling nervous. Her homegirl was sitting with her, and she looks like she be with the shit sometimes, so I know I had to come correct.

I'm a well off guy. I got a lot of shit going for myself and having her on my arm would only add value to everything else. I had to step to her. I got tired of looking at her from across the room.

She had the prettiest smile and beautiful skin. Looking like it was kissed by the sun. Her hair was up in a bun, but I could tell it was really long because her bun was big as shit. It was just something about this woman that had me intrigued, and I had to see where the night would take us.

I asked the waitress to give me two of whatever they were drinking. Approaching, the table with the drinks in my hand, I introduced myself and gave a drink to the young woman sitting with her, and I gave the other one to Cookie.

I'm usually not this forward, but I had to get her to a place alone so I could get to know her better. Did I think she would say yes so quickly? Hell no! Nevertheless, she did, and I was happy as hell. We walked out of the restaurant and got into the car.

"What's a beautiful woman like yourself doing being single? I'm sure men are falling at your feet," I asked as I watched her get comfortable in her seat.

"To be honest, I'm not single." She turned her head away from me like she was ashamed.

"I'm not here to judge you. Apparently, something is not going great because you wouldn't be here with me right now. I'm sure you just don't leave off with strange men often," I responded.

I saw an open park by a big river, so I decided to pull in so that we could get some fresh air and talk. I parked the car, came around to her side, and opened the door for her. Reaching my hand out to her, I helped her get out of the car. It was a little chilly outside, so I grabbed my coat from the back seat and placed it gently around her shoulders.

We walked along the bank of the river until we finally took a seat at this bench that faced the river.

The way the moonlight made her face glow had me in a trance just staring into her eyes.

"You want to tell me about your husband?" I asked.

"I don't want to bore you with my problems, besides it's nothing that I can't handle and eventually get through."

"I understand all that, but I'm asking you. Maybe if you let some of it out, it would help with the pain that you are feeling. I can look at you and tell that your heart is broken. Not sure what he did and if things will get better in your marriage, but I'm here right now just to listen— and not judge!" I added. The last thing I want her to do is to think I'm here to pass judgment on her or anyone. My life isn't perfect, but I make the best of it.

Don't think I'm some soft ass man either; I just know how to approach a woman that has been broken down to her lowest point. I'm not here to break her more, only to help her put the pieces back together, even if it's only for one night. For one night, I want her to feel like she's whole again. For one night, I want her to know that the world is not against her.

"I've been married for two years now. At first, things started off perfect. He was literally my everything. We laughed, we communicated, we took trips, we went to church, and we were inseparable." She paused, and I watched the tears start to roll down her face.

"Lately, I haven't been that special person he once saw me as. I've been cursed out and called everything but a child of God. It really hurts me knowing that my marriage is crumbling and there's nothing I can do or say to make things right again."

"I know you don't know me and my words may mean nothing to you, but never let anyone bring you down to your lowest point. That's your husband, and I get that, but that man took vows to love you through all of this— through the pain, the ups, the downs, everything. Talk to him and see what's going on. The last thing you need to do is stay in a marriage that hurts more trying to keep it together."

I didn't want to come off as the guy who just wants to sleep with her. Although she is fine, I respect her honesty, and the last thing I will do is make her feel any type of regret the next morning for doing something she only did because she was vulnerable.

15

"I think I should go. I've cried too many tears out here with you, ruining your night, and my make up."

"It's ok. You're beautiful without it." She smiled at me, and it took a lot for me not to lean over and kiss her. We got up and walked to my car.

"How can a perfect stranger be there for me and my husband can't?" she asked as we pulled off from the river banks.

"Now that's a question you might want to ask your husband. Just in case he tells you something you don't want to hear, make sure you take my number. Call me whenever you need someone to talk to. I fly back out to Miami in the morning, but I will only be one call away."

I turned the radio on, and we listened to slow jams until we made it to her car.

"Thank you for listening!" she stated, as I walked her to her car.

"It's not a problem Mrs. London Cookie..."

"Bridges," she replied.

"Really? Your mother really named you London Bridges?" I chuckled and caused her to laugh and hit me on the shoulder.

"That's not funny; I guess she really liked the nursery rhyme. Trust me I was teased a lot in school. I must have heard. *London Bridges falling down, falling down,* all throughout the day."

"So I take it once you got married you never changed your last name?"

"No, I kinda like my name how it was, so I didn't think the name change was necessary. The ring and the marriage license was enough for me," she replied.

"Talking about the ring that you're not wearing."

"Yea, I just left out in a hurry, that's all! It's usually on."

"Hey," I held my arms up in surrender style, "no need to explain anything to me. We're good this way." She laughed and slid her hand in her back pocket.

I helped her into her car and watched her as she drove away.

***

Pulling back up to my house in Miami, I dropped one suitcase off and grabbed the other one so I can catch my next flight out.

RING RING

"Yea," I spoke as I answered the phone.

"I got your money, boss man."

"Aight sexy Lexi, I will see you in a minute. I'll come by on my way to the airport."

"Where are you headed now boss man?"

"You know I'm always out here getting this money by any means necessary. I got Tonya out in LA, so I have to meet her to make sure everything is going good with her. She's always getting into some shit with the clients."

"I don't know why you keep her on the payroll," Lexi replied. She always had an issue with Tonya. Tonya brings crazy money in, so I have to keep her on my team.

"Now we both know Tonya is the best at what she does. She keeps the team afloat, especially since yo ass went and got knocked up. We know you won't be able to work for too much longer," I stated.

"Boss man, I'm working up until I deliver. You know these men pay top dollar for pregnant pussy." She laughed, but that was the truth. I have men requesting her and willing to pay whatever she wants.

"You're right! I'ma holla at you though, I will be there in a minute." I hung up the phone with her and laid across my bed a minute.

I know you guys are thinking I'm on some other shit, but I'm not. I'm a good guy, I promise.

Chapter 3

Cookie

After getting back in my car, I went over to my cousin British's house like I told Brandon I would do. I must have laid down for all of 15 minutes before I started hearing her headboard hitting up against the wall. I grabbed my keys and got the hell on down.

2:00 a.m.

Walking into my house and the smell of perfume hit my nose like Ike hit Tina. My heart instantly dropped down into my stomach. I just knew he had a bitch upstairs in my bed. Grabbing the bat from behind the door, I ran up the stairs. I could hear the shower running in our bathroom, swinging the shower door open only to see him in there alone.

"What the fuck is wrong with you, Cookie? Close that damn door letting that cold ass air in here!" he yelled out to me, and I quickly closed the door and sat at the end of my unmade bed.

Looking around the room, I still could smell her perfume lingering around. Tears started to fill up in my eyes.

"I thought you were staying at British's house?" he asked, walking out of the bathroom with a towel wrapped around his waist.

"I decided to come home instead. It didn't feel right sleeping in someone else's bed. Why are you taking a shower so late? Are you just now getting in? And what is that damn smell?" I popped off question after question, hoping to get a truthful answer.

"Yea the meeting ran over a little longer than expected; I just made it here maybe 20 minutes ago and as far as the smell... I thought it was you," he lied. I knew he wasn't going to tell the truth.

I made the bed up before I left to go with British, and he was already gone at that time. He says he just got home 20 minutes ago, so I'm guessing he got in the bed first then decided to take a shower. The shit's not adding up to me.

"Oh ok, I guess," was all I could get out.

The words were there, but nothing would come out. Trying to keep the peace in my house, I go and take a shower and get in the bed beside my husband. I don't know how to approach him, especially since I didn't catch anyone here.

As I laid my head down, all I could smell was Chanel No 9 on my pillowcase, and I knew it didn't belong to me. My heart instantly started racing. I started seeing red, and the devil dancing around my bed. I wanted to hurt his disrespectful ass so bad. Instead, I moved his arm from around my waist, went downstairs into the kitchen and grabbed my phone out of my purse. The only person I knew to call was the perfect stranger. Just from that little time spent with him, I knew he would listen if no one else did.

It's weird to feel a connection with someone who you just met less than 24 hours ago. I knew British was probably knocked out right now and he did say call anytime, so here it goes.

Scrolling to his phone number, I decided just to send a text since that was the quietest form of communication, especially at this hour.

Me: Hey, are you asleep?

Chase: For you, I can lose sleep. What's wrong?

I was surprised by the quick response, but happy that he was up.

Me: Just needed someone to talk to and was wondering if you had a moment to listen. Maybe I am just overreacting to some things. Maybe my mind is playing tricks on me, but I just really needed to vent to someone, and I knew you said I could talk to you anytime.

Chase: Of course you can. If it's about your husband all I'm going to say is just get away for a little while to clear your head. You may need time alone to figure out where you really want to be and if your marriage is worth saving. Honestly, you don't even have to go into details on what's going on. Just take you a mini vacation. Get out of that country ass town and get some sun in your life.

Me: That would be nice, but I don't have anywhere to go. I have tons of papers to grade and test to prepare for my students next week.

Chase: I live in this beautiful city. All you have to do is say the word, and I will send you a ticket. I will keep my hands to myself (Scouts Honor) lol.

Me: Lol, I will keep that in mind. I will let you get some rest and call you tomorrow. Goodnight/Morning

Chase: No problem, Mrs. London Bridges.

I erased the messages, put my phone on the charger in the living room, and went back upstairs.

SMACK!

As soon as I stepped on the top step, Brandon hit me with so much power it nearly knocked me back down the stairs.

"You think you just gone sneak out the room and talk to another nigga in my house!" he screamed and looked down at me with cold eyes.

"Brandon baby, I wasn't talking to anyone. I went downstairs to get a drink of water, that's it!" I yelled back while holding my throbbing face. The pain struck me like lightening, and all he did was turn around, slammed the bedroom door, then locked it.

Slowly, I made my way into my guest bedroom. I just laid there crying and asking God over and over again "why me?". I could not believe he actually put his hands on me.

"I don't know when I became so weak, but God I pray for Strength to leave, Direction to figure out where I'm going, and Protection for him if he put his hands on me again. This is the first time he has ever put his hands on me, and I promise you, it will not happen again. I promise you that!" The more I prayed, the more the devil started talking to me. I prayed harder, and he would talk louder.

The devil won this round.

One thing my dad always taught me is never let a man put his hands on you. I remember he would say, *"Call me first, then pick up something around you and beat the fuck out of him, until daddy arrives."* Ain't no calling daddy this time. I'm sick of Brandon. He put his hands on the right one this time.

I got out of bed, went into my closet where I keep all of my childhood things, as well as things passed down from a deceased relative. My Papa Leroy had this cow whip that my Mama Ida gave me. You know how your parents used to tell you to get your own switch off the tree. Well, this was a switch times ten of any switch you could find. It was very long, thick, and if I swing it right, it would wrap around his ass like a swaddled baby.

I kicked the bedroom door in, since he felt the need to lock me out, and snatched the covers off his naked ass body. He jumped up out of bed ready to charge at me, and I whipped his ass like he was my son, and I just caught him walking around the house in my panties.

"If *whap* you *whap* ever *whap* put *whap* your hands on me again, we're gone have a real fucking problem. *WHAP!*

Every time I spoke a word, I hit his ass. Just looking at him in the corner, balled up like a little baby, gave me more strength— strength I never knew I had. I continued to beat that nigga ass, for the old and the new.

Looking down at him, I saw whelps and some open cuts on his legs. I ran to the bathroom and grabbed the clear alcohol. Not the green shit, I wanted this to buuuurn. I opened the bottle and began talking to him.

"I will tell you this once, and once only! Never ever, ever put your hands on me again, or the next time yo ass is gone wake up dead. That weak bitch that once laid next to you is gone. You woke the beast up in me when you smacked fire from my ass. Every day that I wake up and see this bruise is still on my face, you better hope and pray that my whip ain't by me, or I'm going to beat that ass again. I'ma give yo ass the whooping, ya dusty wig wearing ass mammy should have given you as a child!" I screamed, with much penetration in my voice. I wanted his ass to not only hear my words but feel them motherfuckers too.

"Okay Cookie, STOP!" he yelled out like a defeated bitch, but I wasn't hearing that shit. I started splashing alcohol all over his body. The sounds of his screams made my face feel better. The more he screamed, the bigger the smile came across my face.

Once the bottle was empty, I sat it on the nightstand next to my bed. I pulled the covers back and laid my Cow Whip on the pillow right next to me and went to sleep; and dared his ass to get in the bed with me.

***

Waking up to the smell of breakfast made me jump out of bed quickly. I put on my house shoes and ran down the stairs. My husband never cooks so now I'm thinking someone like that crazy chick from *Thin Line Between Love And Hate,* is in my damn kitchen.

Flying around the corner, I stopped instantly in my tracks once I saw what was on the table. Brandon was standing at the stove scrambling eggs, and on the table, he had fruit, bacon, pancakes, and freshly squeezed orange juice.

"Ahhh umm," I cleared my throat so he could turn around.

"Good morning, princess. I thought I would make you a nice breakfast so you can get your day started out properly. I made plans for you and British to go to the spa, the beauty shop, and a little shopping spree on me," he stated as he ushered me to my seat.

I couldn't help but to noticed the multiple Band-Aids covering his body. It made me chuckle on the inside at the sight of them. *You mean to tell me all I had to do was whoop his ass to get him to act right,* I thought to myself. He made my plate and just sat there and watched me eat.

"You didn't poison my food did you?" I questioned.

"Don't be crazy, London. You know I would never do anything like that. I just wanted to make sure you had enough to eat first, and then I will eat whatever is left over."

"Just eat; I'm sure I won't even eat half of this."

He started fixing his plate and sat on the far end of the table as if he was scared to sit next to me,

I guess a little ass whooping would put fear in even the biggest man's heart.

After finishing my food, I went upstairs to get dressed. I'm still pissed at him, but that's not going to stop me from spending all of his money today.

Picking up my iPhone 7, I called up British.

"Hey love, get dressed. I will be there in a few to pick you up."

"You don't have to tell me twice!" British replied and ended the call.

I put on some cut off shorts, a red v-cut Polo t-shirt, and on my feet, I threw on my red Huaraches. I plan to do a lot of walking going from store to store, so I need to be as comfortable as possible.

Walking down the stairs, Brandon is standing at the door with flowers and his black card. He tried to kiss me on the way out, but I just grabbed his card and kept walking. This new him is only temporary; I am not even falling for this trick. Either the ass whooping helped, or he fucked a bitch in my house last night, and he feels guilty.

Jumping into my car, I made my way towards British's house. I already know her ass is going to be overdressed. She acts like she doesn't know how to dress down when she leaves out the house.

Pulling up, I started blowing my horn to let her know I was outside. She came out with some distressed shorts on that were completely ripped up in the front with a white crop top and some high heels. This lil' girl is always in "I'm ready to take your man" mode. I pressed the button to let my passenger window down.

"Bitch, if you don't go take them damn heels off. We are going shopping British, get comfortable."

Biiitch, hush! Just cause yo ass can't walk all day in heels does not mean I can't; I got this," she replied as she got into the car. "And why are you looking all happy and shit? Ole boy must have put it on you last night," she stated, causing us both to laugh.

"Girl, I did not have sex with that man. We just talked, mostly about my marriage. He seems like a great guy, honestly."

"Let me get this straight. A lonely woman meets a fine man, and the only thing you could find to talk about was your marriage?" She shook her head and applied more lipstick.

British doesn't know what it is like to be married. She's 25 years old, no kids, light skin, nice plump lips, with long hair. She's what you would consider slim thick. All she had to do was bat her lashes in the right direction, and she has all of her bills paid and a couple of bundles.

"Again all we did was talk, which is something he didn't mind doing. He did what Brandon failed to do daily. He didn't touch or kiss me, he just listened."

I smiled just thinking of him. Chase was everything a woman could ask for. He didn't pressure me into doing anything. He just wanted to get to know London.

"Dat nigga is gay," she blurted, catching me by surprise. "Don't laugh, I'm for real! Any other man would have jumped at the sight of seeing a half-drunk woman, especially if she decides to leave with him. He's gone get them draws off one way or another."

"I promise you he was a real gentleman the entire time. But listen to this, once I made it home to Brandon, I just knew that he had a bitch in my house. All I smelled was perfume throughout my damn house. When I laid my head down on my pillow, it smelled like a bitch had just rolled off it before I walked in."

"I know you went ham on his ass. If only I were a fly on the wall honey, yassss!" she spat.

"Actually, I went downstairs, and I talked to Chase. He told me I needed to get away for a little while just to clear my head. He offered to buy me a ticket to Miami, and I told him I would think about it."

"I hope you are done thinking. I would have instantly told his ass HELL YEA! And I would have been on the beach sipping out of a fucking coconut, a pineapple, hell I'll drink out of a shoe, as long as I was away from Brandon ass."

This bitch is crazy, but she's right, I should've said yes, If I had known I was going to get the shit knocked out of me as soon as I went back up the stairs.

"British, when I got back up those stairs that nigga almost knocked my ass out."

"And you should have called me; I would have been over in a heartbeat. He knows I don't play about you, and I told him when y'all first got married to never put his hands on you. Just wait till I see his pop-eyed ass, I'ma buss him dead in his shit!" she exclaimed.

"Pipe down; you already know I handled his ass. Do you remember the cow whip Papa Leroy used to have? I beat his ass with that bitch."

"FUCK DAT YOU SHOULD HAVE CALLED UNCLE DEWAYNE ON HIS ASS!" she yelled, speaking of my father. He plays no games when it comes to his daughter.

"He woke up this morning with a new attitude, cooked breakfast, cleaned the house, gave me money to take me and you to the spa, salon, and shopping."

"That's cool, I will take his money, but I still don't fuck with him. That nigga is on my 'unfuckwitable list' and he ain't coming off. I know you are a teacher and all, but bitch, unfuckwitable is a damn word before you try to correct me."

I couldn't help but laugh at her ass. Again, she's crazy, but I love her. She and I can fight all day long, but if another motherfucka even tries something with me, she is definitely jumping in first.

Chapter 4

Brandon Hamilton

"No, she didn't suspect a thing. She did ask what that smell was though. I told you about wearing perfume over here anyway, especially that kind. She has had her eye on it for a little while now. I told her she didn't need it because she has a dresser full of perfume she rarely wore. So, for you and my safety, keep Chanel No 9 away," I stated through the receiver.

"I hear you. I didn't even have on that much, and I thought for sure it would be gone by morning when she came back home anyway," she replied.

"Yea, but the thing is she didn't stay over her cousin's house. She came home maybe 15 minutes after you left."

"Oh, damn. I'm glad I didn't stay longer for round three. Yo ass had me tired as hell."

"Yea, my dick is good, huh!" I exclaimed.

"Always has been, boo."

"You're fucking right, but shit, let me get dressed. I will see you at the shop later on."

I hung up the phone and finished putting away the dishes. As I walked around the house, I made sure not to let anything touch my wounds. That damn Cookie beat my ass like Jamie Foxx did that white man in *Django*.

It's the middle of May and the temperature supposed to be in the 90s. I went into my closet and pulled a shirt and some pants out of the back. Taking another shower was the last thing I was about to do with all these whelps and shit on my body. Putting soap on me would only cause more pain. I literally looked like I have been beaten like a runaway slave. She made my ass sleep in the corner, and she slept with the cow whip. Where she got that shit from is beyond me, but that shit hurt like hell.

Yes, cheating is bad, but getting a divorce is the last thing on my mind. Cookie is a good woman— matter of fact Cookie is a great woman. It's just we have been making love, and fucking, because those are two different things, for so long it started to get boring. The same position, the same sounds, me pretending it's someone else only so I could hurry up and cum. I would close my eyes and picture her, but when I open my eyes and see Cookie or hear her moans instead of my sidepiece's moans, I get angry. Instantly, I start fucking her harder, not for her pleasure, but I wanted to punish her ass for not being who I wanted her to be. Don't believe that shit you see on TV either, that Abracadabra shit does not work. I've said that shit so many times only to pull the pillow off her face and see it's still her sleeping next to me.

Don't get me wrong my sidepiece doesn't look better than Cookie, but we just have a connection like no other. Her pussy grips my dick with every stroke of it. She's always dropping down to her knees at the first sight of me. Overall, she's a freak and Cookie isn't. I am a man, and at the end of the day, I HAVE NEEDS.

Grabbing my keys off the kitchen counter, I jumped into my 745 BMW and cruised to my shop.

"Good morning," I spoke to my barbers as I walked in the door.

"Issa hot morning boss, so why you got that damn long sleeve polo on and some thick ass sweat pants?" my barber Jonquill asked.

"Maannn, my eczema and this Mississippi heat doesn't mix. It makes my ass itch and breakout worse," I lied. There's no way I was about to tell them my wife whooped my 6'1 200 pound ass like I was a disobedient child.

"I hear you, boss man," he replied sarcastically like he knew I was lying.

I walked to the back into my office, grabbing my clippers and smock, and came back on the floor to wait on my first client.

I only have a few heads today then I'm headed to the new shop to talk to my business partner some more. We need to go ahead and finalize these plans. I want this shop up and running by August. Reaching over to turn the fan on, I grabbed a piece of paper off the counter to fan myself. It was starting to get really fucking hot in here.

"Say B, it wouldn't be so damn hot if you didn't have on all those damn clothes!" Jon B yelled out.

"Fuck you, bruh." I pulled the sleeves up to my elbows hoping no one would notice my bruises. The door of my shop came open, and it was my client, Amber. She came in to get her fade touched up.

"What's up, B?" She dabbed me up, pulled her crouch up like a nigga, and took a seat. Amber kind of puts you in the mind of Young MA, but she cut all her hair off last week.

As I turned her chair around to the front to get her line up right, I forgot about the scars on my arms.

"Fuck bruh, who attacked yo ass like that?" she questioned, referring to the scratches and bruises on my arm.

"I did, trying to scratch myself when my eczema started to bother me," I lied again.

"Nah, I got eczema, and my shit doesn't look like someone took a switch off their mama tree and beat my ass with it, either that or you got mauled by a fucking mountain lion," she blurted out and started laughing.

"Daaamn B, Cookie must have fucked yo ass up!" Jonquill joked as he started pulling on my arm to look at it closer.

"Get the fuck back man; don't you have a client sitting in your chair? Keep playing and all y'all asses that's laughing gone be unemployed and you Amber, yo ass is gone have a half done haircut!" I spat, getting real irritated with them.

I hurried and finished her cut and told Jon B to take my appointments for the rest of the day.

I pulled my phone out of my pocket as soon as I got in my car.

Me: Let's meet at the shop now.

SP: Let me shower and I will be there in 30.

I put my phone back on the holster and headed to my other shop.

Shortly after getting there, I heard keys jingling to open the door. It was my business partner. She started walking over towards me looking so damn sexy. As soon as she got close to me, she started pulling her T-shirt dress off, only to reveal she didn't have any panties on. I pulled my shirt off while she tugged on my belt with so much aggression. She pulled my man out and started sucking my shit like she was about to do 20 years to life, with no possibility of parole and this was the last dick she would see.

"Damn baby girl, now that's how you suck a dick!" I exclaimed.

I put my hands on her head and started fucking her throat. I tried to put my dick so far in the back of her head that it looked like my dick was playing peek a boo with her brain. She started pulling away to regain control. She looked at me with so much passion in her eyes and began sucking on my balls gently. I have never had a bitch deep throat my shit like she does. You would think the bitch was doing a magic trick the way she made my meat disappear.

"Fuck, if I weren't married already, I would be marrying yo ass right now!" I announced.

I placed her on top of the counter, the taste of her pussy is better than any meal I have ever eaten. As I licked and sucked on her clit, she tried to run away, but I wrapped my arms around her thighs so she could not move. I made her sit there and let me feast on her like she was a Ryan's all-you-can-eat buffet. Moments later, she started to cum in my mouth continuously, and I made sure I sucked all of it up. Her legs started shaking, and her body was moving back and forth. Once she came the last time, she put this deep ass arch in her back. I placed my hands around her waist and gently caressed her, pulling her closer to me.

I came up and started moving my dick around the folds of her lips, giving it a gentle massage before I went crazy in it. Aggressively pulling her from the counter to the barber chair, I bent her over and started beating her pussy up from the back.

Smacking her ass only made her pussy get wetter. She became wetter and louder the more I smacked it. She started throwing her pussy back at me and clinching her pussy muscles making it grip my dick like a tight glove.

"Shit daddy, you feel so good," she whispered in my ear, and that made me start going harder until I released my seeds all in her.

"Move out the way," I stated as I gestured for her to move from in front of the chair so I could sit down and catch my breath.

She stood up looking at me with even more lust in her eyes and started sucking me off again. I couldn't do shit but lay my head back and take it. The popping of my toes echoed throughout this empty ass shop. She had a nigga toes curled up like some curly fries from Arby's.

"Hmmm, what's got you all rowdy today? You have never fucked me like that before, Big Daddy."

"I needed to release some pressure, that's all. I was craving your sweet stuff, and I just had to have you," I mumbled as I gave her a kiss on the lips and started to get dressed.

"Damn, what the fucked happened to you?" She started examining my body with this frown on her face.

"Nothing, I had an allergic reaction to shellfish, and it made me whelp up and start itching. I was scratching myself too hard I guess." Another lie!

"Hmph," was all she said, grabbing her purse and started walking towards the front of the shop. "Call me later, I'ma need another round," she announced before exiting the front of the shop, and I left out the back.

I hit my alarm and jumped in the car. Traffic was smooth on today, so it took me no time to make it home. Cookie's car was already parked in the driveway when I pulled in. Entering the house, I saw her and British were sitting on the couch watching reruns of *Martin*, laughing like they ain't ever seen that shit before.

"Hey you're off early, I thought the shop was usually really busy on Saturdays?" Cookie questioned.

"It usually is, but I wasn't really feeling it today, so I had Jon B take the rest of my customers," I replied, continuing to walk past her so I could go upstairs and shower.

SNIFF! SNIFF!

She started sniffing the air and looking around crazy. I continued to walk upstairs ignoring whatever she was doing until she started talking.

"Chanel No 9!" she stated, causing me to quickly turn my head back towards her while still walking. I became nervous as hell and prayed her whip was still in the bed. The last thing I need is for her to beat my ass in front of big mouth ass British.

Hurrying in the bathroom to turn the shower on, I didn't even wait until the water was hot before I jumped my ass in. I grabbed my Dove Men for sensitive skin shower gel since anything else probably would have burned my open wounds. After showering, I threw on some basketball shorts, a wife beater, and laid across the bed, praying tonight is better than last night. For some reason, her actually standing up to me turned me on, but shit, I could not get in the bed; Mr. Cow Whip took my damn place quick. I turned the television on, and before I knew it, I drifted off to sleep.

Chapter 5

Cookie

After spending the morning and most of the afternoon with British, I decided to come home and chill. We did not get a chance to go shopping, but you best believe I still have that card in my purse. We had our wine out and a few snacks just sitting back watching TV. Brandon usually never comes home early on Saturdays because that's when he made the bulk of his money. When he walked past me, all I smelled was the same fragrance that was left on my pillows early this morning.

I guess this nigga didn't learn his lesson last night. But today, I choose not to even entertain him. I grabbed my phone and texted Chase.

Me: I think I wanna take you up on that offer.

Chase: Just say the word lil' mama, and I will have the ticket waiting for you at the airport.

Me: Tomorrow! I will take a few days off work. It's almost summer anyway. I need my break to start a little early.

Chase: Gotcha. It will there waiting on you. Oh and don't bring anything but your purse. I GOT YOU!

"What or who has got yo ass over there smiling like that?" British asked.

"Girl, my mystery man Chase!"

"OOOOH OK... let me find out!" She laughed and grabbed her purse. "Come on girl, drop me back off. I've got bae coming over in a few. I told him we just left the wax lady and he wants to inspect it himself to make sure she did her job properly."

"Aww shit, he's a fool, I see!" Picking up my purse off the table, I said, "Let's go girl." I grabbed my keys, and we headed out the door.

I needed to stop for gas first, so I pulled into the store around the corner. Walking inside to pay for my gas and to grab a root beer, I bumped right into my bestie Noelle when I turned around from the cooler.

"Hey, hoe!" I spoke to her in an excited tone. I haven't seen her since she left to visit her family. "I heard you were back in town. I guess I wasn't good enough for you to let me know that, huh?" I questioned.

"Don't do that, you know I always got time for you. I was handling business, and it slipped my mind to let you know I made it back from South Carolina safely. I'm sure you got other shit going on anyway," she added.

"Nah, I really don't. How is your grandma doing? I know she was happy to see you."

"She's good, taking it one day at a time." Noelle's grandma just found out she had breast cancer so every few months she flew up there to visit her.

"Well, let me go, I have my cousin outside in the car. Call me when you are free so that we can have drinks."

"Yea, I will do that!"

I leaned in for a hug as I always do when we depart each other, I notice her kinda pull back from me as if she didn't want me to hug her. The smell of her perfume ran up my nose, so I pulled back a little from my embrace and just looked at her sideways.

"You smell nice," I stated.

"Thanks, my boo bought it for me; it's that Chanel No. 9 I believe. I don't know for sure, but I love the smell of it on me."

"Hmm yea, it does smell good, I see it has a long lasting effect too," I stated, as I turned to walk off so I could pay for my items. I pumped my gas and left back out towards British's house.

I couldn't help but to notice how my husband and Noelle had matching perfumes on. Now either he's turning into a bitch nigga, or he's fucking Noelle.

I still could not shake how she didn't want to hug me. The lil' bitch was really acting funny towards me, and I know I have been a damn good friend to her. This makes my ass wish I never helped her out that day I popped up at her house when we were kids. I started thinking back to that day, wishing I could take it all back.

"Hey mama, I will be back in a little while, Noelle isn't answering her phone, and we need to get working on this science project before it is too late!" I yelled out to my mom as I grabbed my phone and books off the kitchen table.

"Ok London, tell her mom I said hey."

I closed the door and made my way down the steps of our porch. Noelle only lived five houses down, so it wasn't a bad walk at all.

"Heeeeey London, witcho extra thick ass!" Mike from my third-period class yelled out from the passenger seat of his brother's Monte Carlo.

"Hey, Mike," I answered back in a very dry tone, and placed my headphones around my head, indicating I did not want to be bothered. However, that still didn't stop his ass from getting out of the car and following behind me.

"Why you gotta act like that towards me, L-boogie? You know you want me, girl." Although Mike is a fine lil' chocolate specimen, it does not change the fact that he used to fuck with Noelle, and I ain't never been that type of girl.

"Mike, you already know why I can't get down with you like that." I popped my bubble gum and kept on walking, thinking he would leave me alone.

"L, you and I both know that Noelle is community property. We only got down once and that's it."

I could not do anything but shake my head at him cause I know for a fact he fucked her more than once. Matter of fact, I read messages from his ass begging for more.

"I understand all that, but I'm good on you, playboy."

I started walking up her steps, and his ass sat down on the steps like he was waiting on me to come back out. Mike is a dope boy. Yes, even in high school, he still sells that shit right under the teacher's nose. Outside of school, he kept a gun on his ass cause he already knows it's some grimy ass niggas out here just waiting to catch him slipping.

Walking inside the house, no one was in the living room, so I made my way to the back of the house where her room was located. The closer I got to the door, I heard a muffled Noelle scream out, STOP!

The door was slightly opened, and I peeked inside. I covered my mouth with one hand so they could not hear me gasp for air in shock. What I saw was not what I wanted to see. She was tied up to the headboard, trying hard to keep her legs closed but she was fighting a losing battle. I felt rage and tears form up in my eyes. I gotta do something, I thought to myself.

I ran back outside and asked Mike for his gun, and he didn't hesitate giving it to me. I looked back, and he was right on my heels headed back in the house with me. At this time, Noelle managed to push the sock out her mouth, and I heard her scream out.

"Mama, please stop! Please," she cried over and over again.

"No, you lil' bitch, you wanna give yo pussy to everybody on the block but won't give it to me. You gone let me taste this pussy voluntarily or I'ma knock yo ass out, then yo ass can't do shit but take it!" she yelled, and then I heard her sniffing on Noelle. "Hmmm, you smell so good!"

When we pushed the door open she had one hand squeezing Noelle's breasts, one hand cuffed under her leg, and was eating her pussy. Noelle had tears running down her face, but when she saw Mike and me all that changed. She was so happy we were there to stop her mom.

"Get the fuck off her, you sick bitch!" I yelled out, making her jump.

Mike ran over to her and threw her on the ground, and I wasted no time putting lead right in her ass. I untied Noelle as Mike ran outside and got his brother so he can find a way to help us get rid of this body. After a few days, we reported her mom missing, and my mom got custody of Noelle. She raised her just like she was her own child.

"Girl, what the hell is wrong with you? We've been sitting at my house for 30 minutes, and yo ass has yet to get out of the car!" British spat, pulling me from my thoughts.

"My bad B, I zoned out! Do you mind if I come up with you? I know you have your dude coming over, but I just want to lay down a bit. Brandon is home, and I really don't want to be around him right now."

"Now you know you didn't have to ask me that, it's cool you can come over here anytime," British stated.

Closing the door behind me, I went into her guest room and laid across the bed. The image of my husband and my friend kept playing in my head over and over again. I'm not certain, but some shit isn't adding up to me. After counting sheep, I finally drifted off to sleep.

"Baby, I'm going to take this last customer then come home after I clean up the shop," Brandon stated through the receiver.

"Ok babe, I will be here waiting on you." I hung up the phone and laid across my bed.

It's late, and I wanted my man home with me as soon as possible, I thought to myself, so I decided to get up and throw on some comfortable clothes to help him clean up the shop.

I jumped in my car and did the dash to the barbershop, using my key to let myself in. I thought for sure Brandon would be up front cleaning, either he was in the back, or he decided to go ahead and leave.

Walking into the back where his office was located, the seductive sounds of a soft moan caught my attention.

"Shhiiiit, Brandon, baby!"

"Whose pussy is this?" he asked.

I heard the smacking sound, which I assumed it was his hand making contact with her ass. I stood there and listened to make sure I was hearing things correctly until I just couldn't take it anymore. Once he asked her if she was going to be his wife and she moaned out yes, I lost it! I pushed open the door, and the sight before me caused me to see red instantly.

"Really bitch, my fucking husband!" I screamed out as I ran over to a butt naked Noelle and started beating her ass.

"Cookie... Cookie... baby stop!" Brandon yelled, pulling me off her. Right when he let me go my fist connected with his eye, and my foot kicked him in his dick.

"Fuck you!" I spat, "Of all people Brandon, of all fucking people you fuck with my fucking friend.

"I'm sorry, I swear, she meant nothing to me!"

"Oh, reeeeaaaallllyy!" I emphasized.

Running back over towards her, I only got the chance to kick her in her face before Brandon pulled me back off her again. The feeling that came over me took over my body and I started spazzing out on him. How could he do something like this to me? I have done everything for this man. I literally bent the fuck over backwards to make sure he was straight.

Tears started forming in my eyes, and I blinked them quickly away trying to be strong. Pulling the gun from my purse that I carried with me when I leave out the house late, I turned around and sent a shot right through her temple because she wasn't using her head when she thought to do this shit.

"Cookie!" he yelled out as I turned to him and sent one right through his heart because he was so heartless to fuck my friend and not give three flying fucks how it would make me feel.

The splashing of water on my face caused me to quickly jump up. I looked up and saw British holding a big ass bucket that was once filled with water.

"Bitch! What the fuck did you do that for?" I questioned, wiping the water from my face.

"Yo ass was in here screaming like someone was killing you and I shook you first, and you didn't wake up. So, I figured this cold ass water would wake yo ass up," she stressed.

Rushing into the bathroom to dry myself off, I took my wet shirt off and threw it at her face, and went into her room for a dry one.

"I gotta go!" I grabbed my keys, headed for the door and rushed home.

Pulling up in the driveway, I noticed that his car was already gone again. Unlocking the front door, I made my way in and up the stairs to my bedroom. I didn't have anything to pack since Chase said not to bring anything, so the rest of the night I'm going to use for relaxation and clearing my head of these fucked up thoughts.

Walking into my bathroom, I started running bath water so I could relax. That dream I had at British's house had me on edge. So many things were running through my mind. Maybe I'm just overreacting and this is all a coincidence. *Yea, that's what this is, just all a little coincidence*, I thought to myself.

Looking under my sink, I pulled out my purple bath bomb and dropped it into my bath water. The warmth of the water caused my body to relax. I laid my head back, closed my eyes, and prayed that morning came quickly.

Chapter 6

Chase

Waking up to the sounds of glasses being clinked together, I looked around I see that my place is trashed from the party I had for the girls last night. A few of my high rollers came through and wanted to pick their girls, so it was only right to throw a party and let them showcase themselves. My girls aren't just ordinary girls they are bad, and they can finesse any man out of anything from money, cars, and clothes. The men I introduce them to are straight ballers, most of them just want to be entertained, have companionship, or have a trophy to take to an important event. There were men of all calibers; I'm talking, NBA, NFL, politicians, rappers, singers, anybody with money, was in my reach.

Some may consider me a pimp, or some may say I run a prostitution ring, but I'm none of that! I'm a businessman, simple as that. I have other side hustles that keep money flowing in also.

"Lucinda!" I yelled out to my maid. Today is the day I pick Cookie up from the airport so the last thing I need her to do is come here and this house is nasty as fuck.

"Don't worry sir, I'm already on it!" she yelled back from the kitchen. The sound of the glasses hitting together must have been her picking them up and dumping them in the trash.

Stepping out of the closet, I threw my shorts and a wife beater on the bed. It's hot as hell in Miami, so you will not catch me in anything more than this unless we were about to conduct business.

I like to keep my business under wraps and definitely a secret from the women I date until I feel they can handle what I do. They seem to get intimidated by the other women since they are always around me and again they are some bad bitches. But me as a man, I would never give my woman a reason to feel like any bitch has more value to my life than she does. So, I try to make that shit clear from the jump but some woman just have it in their heads that all men ain't shit.

I headed into the bathroom to top off my personal hygiene before I head to the airport. I don't want to sound like a bitch but shorty was sexy as hell, and I can't wait to see her. She says her man is fucking up, and I'm here to make shit right for her. She can leave that fuck ass town and move in with me. This five-bedroom four and a half bath house is too much for just me.

***

Waiting at baggage claim where she should be shortly, I saw one of my ladies headed to catch a flight.

"What's up, Candy?"

"Hey, boss man. What are you doing up here?" she asked.

"Waiting on my lady to get off the plane." I already knew she was about to be on that good bullshit when I said that.

"Let me find out my boss man is about to get snatched up. She must be special cause you ain't fucked with a bitch in about two years. Not on no 'she's about to spend a few days' type shit. You're the 'let me catch this nut so you can go' type nigga," she announced.

"Get the fuck on, man" I joked, brushing her off. "You just make sure you come back with my money or we gone have some problems. Enjoy your trip. Tell Damon I said what's up and make sure he runs up a check on yo ass too!" I spat, causing her to laugh.

"You know I always make sure that happens. He knows he's gotta pay to play any games this way. I will holla at you though. Enjoy your new boo."

She turned and walked away, and that's when I saw her walking towards me. She had on these fly ass heels, some tight ass jeans that made her ass visible from the front, her hair was in those big ass loose curls you chicks be rocking, and a shirt that showed off her sexy ass abs. Cookie was truly bad as fuck, and I can't wait to make her my woman officially.

"Hey, sexy face," she said as she walked up to me and gave me the tightest hug ever.

"Hey, lil' mama. I'm glad you decided to come visit me. My house has been real lonely lately, and I needed the company just as much as you needed someone to talk to." She smiled at me, I grabbed her hand, and we walked out of the airport.

Unlocking the doors to my G-Wagon, I helped her in. The first stop was Dadeland Mall to see what she could find for her stay here.

"I'm glad you decided to come visit me. I've been thinking about you like crazy."

"Same here, I've been going through some things so getting away for a while was a good thing to help me clear my head."

"Yea I do understand that I was supposed to be out of town on business, but when you agreed to come visit me, I changed those plans quick. What made you come anyway?"

"Truthfully, my husband! There's only so much a person can take until they reached their breaking point. When I met you that night at the restaurant, you seemed like a breath of fresh air to me. You listened, you didn't judge, you just let me vent, and I loved that about you. That instant connection was crazy. Talking to you felt like we had known each other for five years instead of five minutes. I don't want you to think that you are some type of fallback guy cause that's not the case at all.

"No, I don't think that at all. I'm here to play whatever position you need me to."

She looked over and smiled at me. And all I could think about was how I just had to have her in my life, and not on no 'I'll be here when your man ain't around' type deal either. I want her to be my lady. I can see the potential in her, even if she doesn't right now.

Walking into the mall, at first, she acted all shy and shit like she didn't see anything that she liked. Once I told her, she could have whatever she wanted regardless of the price she went bananas. I just took a seat because she looked like she was going to be a while.

"I'm sorry to keep you waiting. This is the best mall I've been to for real. I didn't want to spend all of your money; so I only got a few things." I counted at least ten bags.

"Just a few things, huh!" I chuckled, "Let's go, ma."

We got up, went to the truck, and headed right to the house. You could tell by the look on her face that she loved the view of everything. Shorty was smiling from ear to ear, and I was smiling just at seeing her.

Pulling up to my gate, I used my fingertip to open the gates up.

"Damn you're balling like that, huh?" she joked, "What you got going on that you need this much security? I'm almost scared to get out the truck."

"Just know that you are always safe with me, and I just like to make sure my shit is safe and secure that all. When I get ready to start a family, I will have everything set up and ready for them. They would not have a care in the world cause daddy's gone make sure they are good and safe. Anybody gets through them gates ain't coming back out— alive anyway."

She looked at me like she was trying to see if I was joking with that part or not. "Come on, let's get inside, I wanna show you the house."

She walked in and instantly dropped her mouth open. I had my shit laid; you can't be a businessman living in some bullshit. I have butlers, maids, and a nanny on standby for when I have my first shorty. I have always thought long term. I built this house knowing one day I will have kids running around in here. We walked from room to room, and from bathroom to bathroom.

I could look in her face and tell she was trying to see how she could rearrange shit already.

"Come on, we have plans for tonight so if you want to take a nap, a shower, or whatever you need to do you can. I will be downstairs waiting on you. Let me know if you need your back rubbed or something," I mentioned before I turned to walk away.

"You might as well just stay. I'm sure I will need you sooner than you think."

She went into the bedroom and started to get undressed. Saying I didn't want to look would be a damn lie, and it's not like she was trying to hide anything either. She walked from the bedroom into the joining bathroom and started the shower water. Looking at her soft silhouette through the mirror had a nigga's dick rocking up. Cookie has this cute little circle birthmark on her right thigh, and her face is surrounded by cute freckles.

Sliding the glass shower door back, she stepped in, and I got pissed because the steam from the shower started to fog my mirror up. I started to sneak in and clean that bitch off real quick. As soon as I thought about going in, I heard her sweet angelic voice call for me.

"Chaaaase!" I snapped out of my thoughts and quickly made my way into the bathroom. She slid the door open and motioned for me to come get in. One thing she didn't have to do was ask me twice.

Getting undressed as fast as I can, I jumped in the shower with her. I watched as the water trickled down her body. Handing me the already lathered up sponge, I start washing her body up for her.

Starting at her neck and slowly working my way down, her body was banging in every way. *This damn sponge was taking all of the excitement out of this,* I thought to myself. Dropping the sponge in the tub, I started rubbing my hands around her body in a circular motion until I made it to her pussy.

Slowly I eased my hand between her legs and started gently rubbing her clit. Letting off a soft moan, I knew I was in the right place. I started kissing on her neck and made my way up to her lips giving her the wettest aggressive kiss I had ever giving anyone. This connection I feel with her is a good feeling. I don't know if this is about to be something she regrets doing by tonight, but as of right now, I'm going to enjoy the moment.

Lifting her up, and wrapping her legs around my waist, I eased my dick inside of her.

"Shit! Chase that feels so good!" she moaned out. Her soapy breasts were pressed against my chest as she had her arms wrapped around my neck. I opened the shower door and walked her to the bed with her still wrapped around my body.

Laying her on her back, I could see her giving my body a once over and biting her bottom lip. She did the *come here* gesture with her fingers while spreading her legs and I dove head first into that pussy. The more I ate her pussy, the harder my dick got.

Grabbing my dick, I started moving it around her clit and slipped it right back in.

"Hmmm shit."

She bit my bottom lip in the sexiest way possible, thrusting her hips up against mine. I was trying my hardest not to nut yet, but thinking about cats and dogs wasn't working. With one last good long stroke, I came inside of her. I thought she would freak out, but she didn't. She just pulled me into her and gave me a long ass passionate kiss.

***

RING RING

The ringing of the phone woke me up from the sex coma Cookie put me in.

"Yea!" I grunted.

"Hey, boss man. I need your help with something. One of my clients refuses to pay me for my time. He only asked for dinner and a movie, and I did that, but now he wants sex. That wasn't the deal! It's Sunday, and you know this is the only day I don't schedule my sex appointments so that I won't feel like a hoe. I'm not about to go to hell for his ass just because he wants to get his dick wet!" Duchess exclaimed.

I eased out of bed with Cookie, because I didn't want her to hear my conversation.

"Where are you at? I'm about to come through. Keep him there!"

"At the Embassy Suites over on East."

"Give me a minute, and I will be there."

I jumped up, threw some shorts on, grabbed my gun, and headed out the door.

Getting in my truck, I did the dash to the location. These men already know how I give it up and the last thing I ever play with is my money and my girls' time. Making my way to the room she gave me, I knocked on the door and waited on her to answer it. After several knocks, the door finally came open slowly, and all I saw was Duchess on the ground holding her lip.

"What the fuck, Brandon? We talked about this shit last month! If you can't keep your hands to yourself and only get what you paid for, then we're gone have a real motherfucking problem. You come up here every month on bullshit, and every month I damn near beat yo ass. Now you up here putting yo hands on her because she won't fuck. Nigga, you asked for her to go on a date and to the movies, that's a stack a piece. She did that, now pay her!" I yelled as I pointed my gun to his temple.

"Aight… aight… my bad. I just thought she was down to do more than that since she showed up in that little ass dress and shit." He went into his pocket and pulled out two stacks. As soon as the money was in her hand, I hit his ass on the head with the butt of my gun.

"Don't eva fucking touch her again or next time yo ass gone be missing. Fuck wit' me and see!" I pulled him up by his collar and punched his ass in the face again.

"Let's go, Dutch!" I called out to her. She hurried and put the money in her purse, and we walked out the hotel room.

Brandon always comes here on that dumb shit. He is one of my regulars and spends top dollars on the girls. The only reason I still fuck with him is because he claims he's going through a divorce, and his wife stop giving him pussy. So, I let his ass slide on some shit, but real talk next time this shit won't be pretty.

"Thank you for coming through to my rescue once again with this nigga. Next time he requests me, tell that nigga I'm dead," Duchess stated, causing me to laugh. She's a fool but anything to keep my girls safe.

"No problem. Now let me get back to my lady friend. She's probably up now looking for me."

"Wait, since you're here, this is your cut." She handed me some money, and we went our separate ways.

Chapter 7

Cookie

Easing my way out of bed, I made my way to the bathroom for a quick shower. Chase was already gone somewhere, so I wanted to take this time for myself. Attempting to stand to my feet, I damn near fell back on the bed. I felt like a newborn calf trying to walk for the first time. He really fucked the shit out of me, and I can't even front like I don't want that shit again before we leave for dinner.

I know this seems bad and two wrongs don't make a right, but shit, everything about that was just right. Not having any true proof that my husband is cheating on me doesn't stop the thoughts from continuously crossing my mind. Thoughts of him being with someone else hurt me, and in a way I kinda want him to feel what how I feel.

Coming home to a stranger in my house was something that happened daily. We don't talk, we aren't affectionate, and my body craves that attention. Chase came along, and in one hour, he made me feel whole again. I have never been so attracted to a man outside of Brandon. But, this is what happens when you don't fulfill your duties as a man, and most importantly, as a husband. Someone can easily come along and do the simple things that you lack and make your woman smile.

RING RING

"Hello," I spoke through my iPhone 7.

"Where the fuck are you at?" Brandon's voice boomed through the phone.

"I am where I am, why? Where the fuck are you?" I yelled back

"I'm headed home from a business trip. Your ass wasn't at home when I came back, so I went on bout my business."

"Brandon, I didn't leave till this morning. You didn't come home last night. That's when I decided to take myself on a business trip. I was tired of sitting at home waiting on yo ass."

"Whateva Cook," he said and disconnected the call.

I don't get how he didn't come home all night and want to call and check me. Where they do that shit at? I played the fool much too long.

The sound of the front door was heard throughout the house indicating someone came in. The door to the room I was in came open and there stood fine ass Chase.

"Glad to see you are finally up, go ahead and start getting dressed we will leave in an hour. Oh, and wear something sexy!" He looked at me, gave me the sexiest smile, and closed the door behind him.

I started pulling out all of the sexy shit I bought while we were in the mall. I held up this cute knee length black dress. It has a gold zipper up the front, deeply cut with a split right in the center, with my black and gold Giuseppe heels. He said sexy, but I still have to keep it classy.

Pinning my hair up so I wouldn't mess up the cute barrel curls British put in before I left, I stepped into the shower and let the hot water run over my body. All of a sudden, something came over me, and I just started crying. The emotions from my marriage had me fucked up, for real. I'm here pretending like everything is fine when I know it's not.

This is wrong; this is so wrong, I thought to myself.

I dropped down into the shower and just sat there and cried. Why couldn't I get my happily ever after with my husband? Why couldn't I have the big white house with a white picket fence? All types of questions came to my mind. The tears filled up in my eyes but were washed away by the shower water hitting me right in the face.

The bathroom door came open, and it was Chase. When he saw me sitting down in the shower, he quickly came and opened up the shower door.

"London, what's wrong? Baby, get up." I could see the concern in his eyes. He reached in and picked me up out of the shower, wrapped a towel around me, and walked me into the bedroom.

"Talk to me, what's the deal?" I paused before anything would come out of my mouth.

"This isn't right; I shouldn't be here with you. I think you are a great guy from what I have seen so far, but at the end of the day, you are not my husband. I took a vow before God to love my husband through any and everything. I need to go and make this right."

"Cookie, it's ok! You don't have to explain anything to me. I will call up my guy and ask him to get you home as soon as possible on his personal plane. Just know if things don't work out for you back at home, then my doors always will be open for you. You deserve to be happy, I know I can do that for you, but I want you to make that decision on your own. So I won't get deep into what I can do for you. Just know I'm always one call away." He leaned in, kissed me on my forehead and walked out the room.

I felt really bad, but I have to follow my heart, and right now, my heart is telling me to get home now and be with Brandon De'Shawn Hamilton.

I started getting my things together and leaving everything that Chase bought me here. Not because I didn't want it, but hell it was a lot of shit to carry on a plane, private or not.

"He will be ready to take you home in 30 minutes," Chase came in the room and stated. "You straight?" he added.

"Yes, I will be. Chase, I'm really sorry about all of this."

"Cookie, trust me when I say we are just fine. If things are meant for us to be then, we will be. I'm not into taking another man woman because I know I would hurt a nigga over mine. And if you were mine I would most definitely kill for yo fine ass," he spoke, causing me to laugh.

"I hear you. I'm actually ready now so just let me know when you are ready."

"Ok, let's go then." We got in the truck and headed right to the airstrip.

***

I made it back in last night, and Brandon was nowhere to be found. He never even came home or called my phone. All of the shops are closed so I had no idea where he would be. So much was running through my mind, and I needed someone to talk to. I called on my best friend Noelle, because she always knows what I should do, plus I wanted to pick her brain a bit. We made plans to meet up at The Grill for Mimosas.

I waited outside maybe 15 minutes before she finally decided to pull up.

"Hey lady, it took you long enough." I stood up and reached out for a hug as I do every time.

"I know, sorry! You caught me in the middle of a session, so I had to clean myself up and get dressed."

"Hmm, a session huh! Who is the lucky guy this time?" It's always someone new in her life. I swear she changes men more than she changes her panties. "You usually always fill me in on the guys, but for some reason, you are keeping this one a secret," I stated as I continued to look down at the menu.

"I know I just don't want to jinx this one, so I'm going to keep him a secret as long as I can. Enough about me how are you and my brother doing?" she asked, trying to flip the subject.

"Not that good, he didn't even come home last night. He has been at that new shop so much, I rarely see him. On top of that…" I hesitated before I started back speaking. "On top of that, I think he is having an affair." I put my head down so she wouldn't see the tears falling. She got up from her seat and sat down next to me.

"Aww baby, don't cry." She laid my head on her shoulder and continued talking, "Shhh, shhh it's ok. You know Brandon; he has always been tied up with his job. Then he is trying to get his new shop off the ground, and I'm sure that's stressful. Just give him a chance to get things settled. He will be back to the old 'crazy about Cookie' Brandon he has always been," she added. Maybe she is right; I can't even imagine how hard it is running a shop and trying to open another one.

"Thanks, I'm sorry for the tears, we supposed to be enjoying our drinks." I grabbed the napkin off the table and began plotting the tears off my face.

"It's ok; you know I am always here for you." We ordered our drinks and food and talked a little while longer before going our separate ways.

I popped the alarm for my car and headed to the house, hoping he was home. Exiting on 18th Avenue, I turned down by the hospital and down my street. I was happy to see his car in the driveway. Grabbing my purse, I rushed out the car and right into the house.

Once I walked in, I was greeted by rose petals and candles everywhere. Stopping in my tracks, I scanned the room until my eyes landed on a naked Brandon lying on the couch with a long stem rose in between his teeth. I don't know what he was thinking, but I was not in the mood for him to fuck the shit out of me and have my shit dry and bleeding.

"What is all this?"

"I just wanted to show you how much I appreciate you. I am sorry for being an asshole lately. I almost got everything squared away with my new building, so I will have more time to give to my wife."

He came over to me and started kissing me, and for some reason, I kept imagining he was Chase. I welcomed the kiss he gave me until he started trying to put his hand in my pants.

"Baby wait, my cycle is on." I lied, I just had sex with Chase yesterday, there's no way I was about to fuck Brandon the day after.

"Shhhh, we can lay a towel down. Just go sit in the tub, and it will stop the bleeding for a little while."

I did as I was told. As bad as I didn't want to, it would look bad if I refused him sex when I never have before. Running my bath water, I got in and tried to stay in until my ass started to wrinkle.

"Damn girl, hurry up!" he busted in the bathroom and stated, still naked. Grabbing my big dry towel, I got out of the tub and headed into the bedroom.

"Come here," he requested and started pulling me towards him and taking my towel off. "Your body is so gorgeous."

The way he was acting, I thought he was about to take it slow with me, but I fooled myself. He snatched my towel off me and threw me on the bed. Without any hesitation, he rammed his dick inside of me and started fucking me with so much force and aggression just like how Ike fucked Tina when she was in the booth recording. His hand was wrapped around my neck, and I was gasping for air, and he continued to fuck me like he was a lunatic. After a few more rough strokes, he came inside of me and got up. I could not do anything but lay there and cry. I was in so much pain I couldn't even make myself get out of bed to shower.

***

2 weeks later

School was finally out for the summer, and I could not wait to get away from these kids. It's not that they are bad, but hell, I was just tired of hearing my damn name being called all day long. Brandon has still been Brandon, not coming home and he has not touched me since that night he fucked the shit out of me. Chase, on the other hand, has constantly been showing me he wants to be with me. He makes it his business to come visit me every week. Brandon has been so wrapped up into whatever that he does not even notice the nights I do not come home, probably because his ass didn't come home those nights either.

Pulling into my driveway from having drinks with British to celebrate our last day as teachers for the next two months, I opened the front door and placed my keys on the table. Looking around, I see that my place is exactly how I left it. Nothing has been touched and no man in sight. I picked my keys back up off the table and went back out the door. It's Friday night, so usually, he goes over to his new shop to tighten up loose ends.

Pulling out of my driveway, I quickly made my way over to the shop. I stopped at the liquor store on the way there so we can have a drink to celebrate him finally closing. Getting out at the shop, I grabbed my wine bottle and my gun. One thing I learned is never to trust these men on the streets. It's late, and I never leave home without her. I placed the gun into the small of my back and made my way across the street to the shop.

Walking into the building, I was instantly hit with the sounds of moans coming from the back. At first, I thought I was tripping, but the moans started to get louder and louder.

Putting the wine bottle down on the counter by the register, I slowly and quietly made my way to the back. It could be his business partner Jon B here with a girl, so I definitely didn't want to fuck up his nut. There was a crack in the door, so I peeked in, and to my surprise, I saw my husband head in between my best friend thighs. She was lying back on his desk completely naked, holding on to his ears like they were fucking handlebars, on a 10-speed bike. I don't know if I was madder at the fact that he doesn't eat my pussy like that, or at the fact that he was cheating on me, and with her.

"Are you fucking serious? After all this time, this is what you do to me, and with my fucking best friend." I announced making them both jump up, and she ran into the corner like how Ebony did on *Players Club*.

I ran over to her and started punching and kicking her ass in the face. I wrapped her hair around my hand so she wouldn't get away with one hand and started feeding my fist to her with the other one. I wanted her to feel me, I could give a fuck about him, but this was my best friend. We've been through it all together, and this is how she shows me her appreciation by fucking another one of my men, lil' rotten pussy bitch.

I guess he got tired of me beating his bitch's ass, so he pulled me off her and threw me back to the wall.

"Oh! So you want to protect her and say fuck me, huh? Ok, I got something for you both." I pulled my gun from my back and pointed it at her first. "Bitch, I have always been there for you. Every time some fuck boy fucked you over, who did you come running to, huh?" She didn't say anything; she just sat there covering herself up in the corner.

"Bitch, you hear me! Now answer me, who was there for you, Noelle? I was, right? Who protected you when yo dike ass mama was trying to bump pussies with yo ass? I was the one who made sure she would never hurt you again. When I came to you crying about my husband and how I thought he was cheating on me, who do you think told me to trust my husband? You did, right? You made me believe everything was all in my head. How I had the perfect fucking husband, and he just needed time because he was getting his other business off the ground and it may be stressful. You made me give him just an ounce of trust. If you were fucking him, you could have said nah just leave him alone, he ain't no good. I would respect that more than you talking me into staying with his dog ass knowing good and gah damn well, you were fucking this nigga!" I spat, I felt like I had fire blowing out of my ears, I was so fucking heated.

"Cookie, I am so sorry. He came on to me first, I didn't mean for this to happen like this, please forgive me." she pleaded.

"I don't give a flying fuck who came on to who, Noelle. Somebody should have had sense enough to say this shit ain't right."

"I know, and I'm so sor..." she attempted to apologize, but I didn't want to hear that shit. She was my best friend, my best fucking friend and she betrayed me. How could she hook me up with a nigga that she knew from the jump, she was feeling.

POW! POW!

I sent two bullets right through her head, making her brain scatter all over the walls and the floor. I was tired of listening to the lies. The truth is, she fucked him because she wanted to. It ain't have shit to do with who came on to who, stupid hoe.

"Cookie, you didn't have to kill her. I'm sorry it wasn't supposed to be like this. Trust me when I say I didn't love her. She was just easy," he explained.

"So all it took was for an easy bitch to come along, and you forget you have a fucking wife. Of all people tho B, you picked her and to think I was actually trying to make shit work with you. I should have stayed where the fuck I was."

"Fuck you mean?" he questioned.

"Oh, one thing you don't have the right to do anymore is question me. I told you not to fuck with me. I said that PLAIN AND FUCKING CLEAR. I have been hurt Brandon, and I don't want to get into a relationship with you if you are going to play games with my heart. You promised me you were different. You promised me that you would never cheat on me, that I would never have to live in my past again. But this is what you do, the exact same thing that they did. Oh but wait, that's not even the fucked up part.

As my best friend, she knew first hand on the bullshit I went through with my ex. Did she tell you she fucked him too? Yea, the bitch really loved my leftovers because she stayed going after them. But, good friend Cookie forgave her ass and started trusting her again. We were young, and mistakes happen. I mean the nigga was 1000 times finer than you, and he had this South Carolina accent that made my pussy instantly wet and his dick was bomb.

I didn't think she was gone go and test it. That was my mistake for telling a bitch about how good my man fuck me anyway, and how this nigga had a 12 gauge sawed off double barrel shotgun between his legs. I gave her a good reason to want to try him. It looks like she did the same thing with you too. I am the reason it's so easy for her to get my men. I talk too fucking much, and I'm too fucking trusting.

Never again will I let a motherfucker get 12-inch dick length to my man before I smack the shit out of her ass."

"Cookie, just give me another chance to show you I can do right by you. Cookie look at me!" he yelled out, "I don't want anyone else." What he said made me laugh my ass off.

"Well, of course not cause the lil' hoe you were fucking with is dead now. Don't worry, y'all going to the same place. She will meet you at the crossroad."

POW! POW!

The gun went off, and his body fell to the floor. I sat down at his desk as tears started to roll down my face. I fired up the blunt I'm guessing he had sitting there until they finished fucking.

Kicking my feet up on his desk, I pulled my phone out of my bra, I texted British first, and then called up Chase.

Chapter 8

British Monroe

I headed out of my bathroom after I just beat my face for my dinner date. I have been watching a ton of YouTube videos, so I finally mastered that contouring shit and my brows actually look like mine. Some of them women shits be looking like they found the biggest Sharpie black permanent marker at Dollar Tree. I'm just saying they be having so many besties but fail to ask them hoes what they really look like. I wouldn't let Cookie walk out the house looking like that.

I walked over to my full-length mirror and gave myself a once over, and yes my ass was looking fat in my high waisted Fashion Nova jeans. I had on some denim jeans, a crop light denim shirt that had a really cute big ruffle going around my shoulders with some bad as heels to match. I had a date with this fine ass man I met that same night Cookie met her mystery man.

He was everything a woman could ask for. Fine was an understatement that nigga was blessed by Mary before God started sculpting his masterpiece. Tank stood 6'2, about 210 pounds, smooth whipped chocolate skin tone, with abs that looked like I could take a load of laundry and just wash them on him. Tank had a nice well-maintained beard. That bitch was so pretty it looked like he put a silk wrapping cap on it at night to keep it proper. You know how they say people have bedroom eyes, well that's Tank, looking into his eyes will make you lay all your burdens down and have your little light shining and shit. That man had it all!

I'm a short girl, and it's just something about a tall man with nice arms that make me feel safe and secure. There ain't nothing a short nigga can do for me but let me sit on his face.

After that first night of being with him, we have been together every day.

"Hey, Big Zaddy," I said as I walked up to Tank, who was standing by the car waiting on me.

"What's good, ma!" Tank said as he opened the door for me.

The car he picked me up in was a brand new 2017 all black Charger; it still had the new car smell to it. Once he closed the door, he leaned over gave me a long juicy kiss with those sexy lips of his and we headed to the restaurant. He took me to this nice steak house, called Ruth Chris, where we had our own little section to ourselves. Candles, wine, and his fine ass was all I needed to top my night off.

"So tell me a little more about yourself. I'm sure it's more to you than that good D you delivered the other night." We laughed together.

"I definitely have more to offer than good D. I actually have a little dating service that I run with my brother back home. I have a few other things going on too, but it's nothing major, I'm always making sure I have money coming in at all times."

"I know it's kinda too late to be asking now, but what about a lady? A man as nice looking as yourself should have a flock of women behind you."

"Nah, I'm solo. I don't be out as much. My ass be in the house like a married man, if I'm not out of town with my brother. Have you ever been to Miami?" he questioned.

"No, but from the way it looks on the TV it seems like a beautiful place."

"You should come visit me one day; I'm always up for company."

"That sounds nice; I think I would really like that." He reached across the table and rubbed the back of my hand. The waitress came over and began pouring me another glass of wine.

"Did anybody ask yo ass to come over here and fuck with us! If she was thirsty, I'm sure she would have waved a fucking red flag, so you could bring yo simple ass over here to give her more wine. Now if you would excuse us, I would like to finish my dinner with my beautiful date!" Tank yelled out at the poor little old lady. She was petrified and shit for a second I was too. I can't even lie like that shit didn't turn me on, though. Call me crazy but if I were wearing panties, they would definitely be wet right now.

He had this evil look in his eyes that let me how that he was batshit crazy, and now I see why his ass is single. Everybody is fucking scared of his big ass.

"What was all that about?" I questioned, once the old lady ran away from our table.

"I don't like to be interrupted. She saw me looking into your beautiful eyes, and here her ass comes pouring wine and shit. Lil' old bitch. LET'S GO; she's ruined my fucking night." He jumped up and threw his napkin on the table along with $200, grabbed me by the arm, and snatched me out of the restaurant.

"Hold the fuck up, you acting a little too crazy for me. I'm good on you homie. I snatched away from him and pulled my phone out so I could call a taxi. He had life totally fucked up if he thought I was going anywhere else with his dumb ass.

"Fuck you then, trick!" he yelled out and jumped in his car as soon as valet pulled up. That nigga was completely off his rocker, and I ain't got time to fuck a nigga up.

Scrolling through Facebook while waiting on my taxi to pull up, a text came through from Cookie."

Cookie: CALL ME ASAP!!!!!

Oh shit, what the hell has happened with her and Brandon crazy ass now.

I called her phone, and she answered on the first ring.

"I fucked up!" she yelled out. I could tell she had been crying by the sound of her voice.

"What happened, Cook? Did Brandon do something to you?"

"When I came here I caught his ass fucking Noelle bitch ass. After that, I just lost all control."

"Fucking Noelle?! That nasty bitch. Where are you now?"

"I'm still at his shop, I don't know what to do British, please help me!" she screamed out.

"Just calm down, text me the address, and I will get my taxi to drop me off there. Just stay calm, cousin."

She never said what she did when she lost control but if I caught my best friend fucking my husband they were gone have to bring several body bags to pick up those bodies. The shit is disrespectful as fuck. It seems like everyone is having a fucked up night.

My date was the date from hell, and his dick is good as fuck, but I can't choose good dick over him acting a donkey in public like that. I'm sure I could find someone else with all of the above that I am looking for.

The taxi pulled up, and I jumped in.

"Take me to 267 Howard Street and fast please."

He stepped on the gas; there was no traffic, so he did the dash all the way there. I threw him a tip and ran to the building. What I saw was definitely not a pretty sight. All I saw was blood, bodies, and Cookie sitting in the chair smoking a blunt with tears pouring out of her eyes. When she saw me, she ran over to me, wrapped her arms around my neck, and cried so hard.

I felt really bad for her. Knowing the man you were married to was fucking your best friend had to be the worse feeling ever. But, from the looks of this room, she got the ultimate revenge on both of their asses.

"Shhhh baby, it's ok!" I rubbed her back trying to calm her down as she cried into my shoulder.

"How could they do this to me? I loved both of them and would do anything for them, and they were laying up here fucking like crazy. On top of that, he was fucking the bitch in my house. I don't smell nothing but that perfume all up in this damn office. Seeing them together caused me to lose all control. After I told that hoe how I felt I blew her fucking brains out and after he had apologized I sent his ass to that special place in hell with her."

The sight of the room was making me real nauseous, so I had to get out of there and quickly.

"Sweetie, look at me. I love you, I really do, but this shit is making me sick to my stomach. I have to get out of here. Do I need to do anything before I go, drag a body out give you a water bucket to clean this shit up?"

"No, I'm about to call Chase and see if he can help me or know anyone here who can. I have to get rid of these bodies and clean this damn place up."

I gave her a tight hug and made my way out the door. Good thing this new shop was only a few blocks from my house. Walking was the best thing I could do to clear my head. Raindrops started falling so I tried to speed up this last block.

SSSSKKRRRT!

The sound of a car jamming on its breaks as I crossed the street caused me to jump back out of the way. The rain had started coming down pretty bad, so I could hardly see. The driver threw the car into park, jumped out and snatched me up. I started kicking and screaming trying to get away from him, but he was too strong for me.

"Shut the fuck up before I give you a reason to scream!" I instantly recognized the voice; it was Tank crazy ass. He had a hoodie on tied tight around his face so I couldn't see it but his voice is so distinctive. He had all of the doors on child lock so as hard as I tried to get out there was no escaping him.

We drove for what felt like hours, and he pulled into this rundown house. He snatched me out of the car and dragged me inside. The house had granite counter tops and nice hardwood floors, but from the outside, it looks like a piece of shit.

Pulling me into one of the bedrooms, he threw me on the bed and snatched my clothes off.

"Please don't do this, can you please just let me go home?" I screamed out, and that didn't even make him flinch. He started taking his clothes off and climbed into the bed with me. Now, I have had sex with him before but that shit was willingly, but this right here is straight up rape.

Throwing my legs open, he dove head first into my pussy, and I couldn't help but release a loud moan. Even though I had tears coming out of my eyes from the fear of not knowing what he would do to me, I couldn't help but moan out with pleasure. He was devouring my pussy, and I was more pissed at the fact that I couldn't enjoy it.

The shit started feeling so fucking good— actually better than it did when I gave him permission. Tank started sucking on my clit, and I felt my body start to shake, and I started to cream all over his face. He used that long tongue of his to lick all around his lips to get the cum off.

Placing a kiss on my pussy, he started kissing his way up my stomach and licking around my breasts.

"Tank, can you please let me go? We can do this the right way where we both can enjoy this," I said, trying to talk him into letting me go. "I would feel much better if I was in my own house, in my own bed. You don't have to continue doing this. If you would just untie me, I will do whatever you want me to do, if you take me ho…"

Before I could get any more words out of my mouth, he had knocked me out cold. When I came to, I was laying in the bed with absolutely nothing on, the sheets were bloody, and my pussy was throbbing. He still had me tied up to the bed, but I didn't see him anywhere in sight.

"Taaaaank… Taaaaaank!" I yelled out, but my cries went unanswered. He had, in fact, left me there tied up to the bed. It was now daytime, and I had no clue where I was at or where in the fuck he was at for that matter.

Feeling something dripping out of my pussy as I threw my legs up and tried to untie myself with my feet, I knew it was either blood or his nut, and I could only pray his ass didn't cum inside of me. The last thing I need is this nigga crazy ass seeds swimming inside of me.

Chapter 9

Chase

That night, after dropping Cookie off at the airstrip I had a lot of free time since plans were changed. I had the entire night planned for her, something that I haven't done for a woman in years. We were going to have dinner, and I planned us a nice little helicopter ride over the city.

Years ago, my wife was killed in a car accident, and I never moved on to another woman. That night I saw Cookie it was something about her that grabbed my attention as soon as she stepped into the building.

She had this certain glow about her that I have only seen my wife have. My wife and I were married early, the age of 21 to be exact. Monica was truly my everything. When I took that vow to love her for better or worse, I stood on that word. I had no thoughts of being with another woman other than my loving wife until now. Even now, I still can't say I want to be with her because she has a situation going on and on top on me not fully being honest with her yet. It's just been me, so I never had to explain my profession to anyone.

Before I started this business, I was a legit businessman. My father passed this shit down to my little brother and me. He is into it a lot more than I am. I make sure my girls are straight and shit, but hell majority of the cut goes to them. 60/40 is my deal, and they get the 60. Eventually, I'm passing all of this shit down to my little brother. This shit was never my cup of tea, even when my father was trying to teach me how to run shit.

If Cookie does make a decision to leave her husband for her own reasons, then before we move forward I will let her know the truth. Building a relationship on a lie won't make it stronger, that shit is bound to fall. I know what I do may not be everyone pick for a job, but hey my girls love what they do, and I always make sure they are straight. The only client I ever had a problem with was Brandon. I met this nigga one day I was in Columbus on business. I had two of my girls with me, and he was staring at them like he wanted a piece. She went and introduced herself to him, and he been burning up some frequent flyer miles coming back and forth ever since.

Pulling up to one of my spots, I called up my head honcho, Charm. When I can't make it to check on the girls in different states, I send her. She doesn't get down like they do, she is strictly about her paper. I like to call her my lil' hitta cause when them niggas are acting dumb with one of my girls she is quick to fuck his ass up. My girls will get their paper one way or another. Either you gone pay what you owe voluntarily, or either we gone fuck you up and take everything, involuntarily.

"What's good, Charmaine?" I stated, getting out of the car and walking up to the house where some of the girls live, and no it's not a hoe house.

"Hey, boss man. I thought you would be tied up a while. Duchess told me you had some company in town for a few days."

"Her big mouth ass! Yea, but she left a while ago, so it's back to business for me."

We walked into the house where Tonya, Marie, and Patrice were. The sight before me had me angry as fuck. "Y'all need to clean this nasty motherfucker up. Ain't no way this house should look like this!" I yelled when I saw it looked like a fucking storm came through. It's a four bedroom house, and neither one of them put money on anything, I do it all.

"I've been in class or in the library studying for my finals, so I'm hardly here to fuck up anything, you might want to talk to Ree and Patrice about that shit," Tonya replied, gathering her books and papers off the living room floor.

"That doesn't even matter tho, all y'all live here, so all y'all clean this shit up."

Like I said my girls aren't all bad. Most of them are in school getting degrees, and this is just a little side hustle to pay for what they need. Tonya only does companionship dates, no sex, just dates and conversation. She's smart as hell, so she finesses these niggas just with her mouthpiece alone.

RING RING

The ringing of my phone stopped me from heading to the back of the house where the other two girls were.

"Hey baby, I'm glad you called," I stated to Cookie as soon as I picked up the phone.

"Chase I need you!" she replied quickly.

"You straight? What's going on? I already know that nigga did something. You should have just stayed here and enjoyed your time with me."

"I agree, but I came home with good positive intentions, but when I got off work today, shit went left real quick. I um... I kinda need your help with something."

"Whatever it is, I got you."

"I hope so. Is there a way you can come here soon? Like really, really soon?"

"Yea, I will see if a flight is leaving out tonight or first thing in the morning. Is that straight?" I questioned. I don't know what's going on, but shit she needs me, so I'm going.

"Yea that's cool, I will be here in the same spot looking at these dead bodies and shit," she mumbled.

"Wait, run that by me again?"

"Nothing, I will see you when you get here. Again, Please try to come as fast as possible."

We hung up the phone, and I told the girls I had to bounce. Turning around, I walked out the house and headed right to the airport. I called up another one of my workers who work at the airport. I needed her to let me get on the first flight out.

***

"Hey love I'm here where you at?" I spoke through the receiver.

"Pulling up right now."

She pulled up in an all black Lexus, and I jumped in.

"What's going on?" I asked as soon as I shut the door.

"When I made it home, Brandon wasn't home, so I decided to go to his other barbershop to surprise him. I walked in to see him fucking my best friend," a tear started to fall from her eyes, and she quickly wiped it away.

"Damn, that's fucked up!" I really didn't know what else to say to her. I have never been in that position so it's not like I can say, oh you'll be fine."

"When I saw them together, I lost all control and before I knew it they both kinda just ended up dead."

"Cookie, no one can just end up dead, what you mean?"

"I mean, I killed her then I killed him. I was angry and lost control of myself now I have to clean this shit up."

"Just calm down, I told you I got you, and you can always call on me. I meant that about any and everything. You made a mess, and I can clean that shit up for you. Let me make a call to my guy here, and we can get this handled for you. Give me the address, and I will send it to him."

Reaching in my pocket, I pulled out my phone and called up my guy Justin. He runs this cleaning crew, and I know he is always down to make some extra money.

We pulled across the street from the shop and went inside. Shit, I know I'm a nigga, but I was almost scared of what I was going to see.

Cookie was just a little bit too calm about the shit like she has done this shit several times before. She pushed the office door open, and I swear it looked like an episode of *Snapped*. The bitch in the corner was beautiful as hell, but those bullets in her body fucked her all up. She didn't even let her put her clothes back on before she killed her ass. My eyes scanned the room and landed on another body on the floor.

"Brandon!" I blurted with the look of confusion on my face. "Daaammmmmn! That's yo husband?" This nigga has been my client for the longest. He mentioned he had a wife, and they were going through something, I had no idea it was Cookie. That's some fucked up shit right there.

"How do yo know my husband?" She quickly turned around and questioned me.

"He is one of my distant business partners." That made no sense, but I didn't know what else to tell her. I didn't want this situation to lead up to me telling her about my business now since she's already pissed off.

"Hmph!" she mumbled.

"Babe, Justin is on his way. I think you should leave and go to a hotel room. Once we get everything squared away here, I will call a taxi or Uber or whatever the fuck they have out here to drop me off. Make sure you text me and let me know which hotel you are in."

As soon as she drove off, Justin and his crew pulled up.

"What's up, bruh. I need you to take care of a little situation I got myself into." We walked to the back of the shop, followed by his cleanup crew.

His crew was in and out and made it look like nothing ever happened. They took the keys to his car and one of the workers left in it. Justin also owns a chop shop so that shit won't be looking like that for long. Once they were almost done getting everything cleaned up, I went ahead and called someone so that I could meet up with Cookie. When I left, Brandon was still there waiting to be removed. They removed the naked bitch first.

***

"You ok, baby?" I rushed in and asked Cookie when I saw her lying across the bed crying. I didn't expect her not to have any feelings towards what happened, so I knew she would break down soon.

"I just wanted you to come here first before going right to your house alone after a situation like that. When Justin gets everything completed, he will be up here so I can pay him." I watched her, and she just laid there on the bed staring off into space; about an hour later Justin knocked on the room door.

"Justin, this is my girl Cookie! Cookie, this is my guy Justin." She stood there like she was in shock for a bit then she finally spoke up.

"Hi... hey, nice to meet you," she stuttered like she was still nervous about what happened.

"Nice to meet you too, Ms. Cookie."

"You got everything handled for us?" I questioned Justin. I met him a while ago when I was on an assignment here, and he was part of the cleanup crew. He seemed like a solid guy, so I always fucked with him when I needed something like this done.

"Everything is good and clean you won't even be able to tell someone lost their fucking minds in there."

I almost knocked his ass out when he said that shit. What type of shit is that to say? I know she wasn't there when he came, but still my nigga you know that shit had to be done by someone else since my ass wasn't fucked up about it at all. I paid his ass and got him the fuck out with all that bullshit he was talking.

"You may want to go to the house to grab some things, and we will leave out in the morning. That's if you want to come back with me. I don't want you to do anything you aren't ready to do."

"Yea, I think that's a good idea. I definitely don't think it's a good idea to stay here."

We left out the hotel and headed to her house. She was quiet the entire way there, and I didn't want to say the wrong shit and be another one of those bodies she got bagged. About 15 minutes later, we pulled up to her crib, and it was nice as hell from what I could see.

She unlocked the door, and we went inside and up the stairs. This house was almost as nice as mine was, minus the bedroom door hanging off the hinges.

"I'm about to take a shower, and I guess we can get some rest until morning," she stated, walking into the bathroom and starting the shower. "Feel free to join me."

One thing you will never have to do is ask me to join you twice. I got undressed and hopped in the shower with her. This probably wasn't the right time, but her body looked amazing with the water dripping off it.

I grabbed her towel and gently washed her back. Giving her a kiss on the neck and sliding my hands around her body to turn her around, she let out a moan as I continued to kiss on her. After we had engaged in a long passionate kiss, I started kissing and sucking on her breasts and making my way down to her inner thighs. Lifting up one leg and placing it over my shoulder, I let my tongue do all the talking for me. Her pussy tasted so good! Hearing her moaning made me go even harder because I knew she was about to cum. I gently worked my tongue around her clit several times, and she pulled my head in closer to her.

"Baby... oh shit... I'm about to cum... ooooohh fuck!!!" she moaned out as her juices started gushing out.

I stood up, and she instantly dropped down to her knees. Most women would complain about their hair getting wet, but not Cookie. The wetter it got, the more her hair started to curl up. I moved her hair from her face and watched as she bobbed her head back and forth on my dick.

"Damn, baby!" I stated as I ran my fingers through her hair with one hand and held onto the wall with the other.

She was making me feel like a real bitch. She deep throat my shit until she gagged, she had spit all over my shit. Just seeing it made my man get harder, I could feel my dick swelling up more and more. Not ready to nut yet, I got out the shower and walked her into the bedroom. I came up between her legs to slide it in, but it was so tight that I had to work my way in gently. She was saying take it slow and that it was hurting, but she still raised her legs up so I could get deep up in those guts.

"You straight, baby?" I whispered in her ear.

"Yes baby, please don't stop."

I began stroking her real slow making her feel every inch of me and tongue kissing her at the same time. I noticed that made her pussy wetter, so I had to make a mental note of that. After slow strokes I came out of the pussy and started slapping my dick on her pretty pussy over and over, then I jammed it back it and went bananas on her ass. I came back out and held her legs up like I was about to change her pamper and started sucking on her pussy. Watching her squirm turned me on, and I had to get back in it. Easing my way back in, she started to moan louder. She wrapped her legs around me making sure I would not pull out again.

"Chaaase, baby oooh shit baby. Baby, baby, fuck I'm about to cum. Daddy, please keep going!" When I felt her pussy get tighter around my dick, I exploded inside of her at the same time she was coming.

"I can't wait for you to tell me your period didn't come cause I know I just dropped a carload of bad ass kids off in you.

***

RING RING
RING RING

"Cookie, baby, wake up, your phone is ringing." I rolled over, but she wasn't in bed anymore. Walking into the kitchen, she was there cooking breakfast in absolutely nothing. It was a definitely a beautiful sight to see.

"Good morning, sexy face. It's good to see you have finally decided to get out of bed. You moaned in your sleep all night," she joked.

"Shit, you had a nigga having dreams about yo ass. You turned me into a real bitch last night," I replied. "I came down here to tell you your phone was ringing, though." Handing her the phone, I watched as she read the text that was on her screen.

"Something isn't right! This is Jon B talking about he got a text from Brandon late last night and asking if I can meet him at Klean Kuts as soon as possible."

"Calm down baby, that was Justin. I tried to make shit not look so fucking crazy with how he and your best friend just end up missing, so I made it seem like they ran away together and tossed the phone. You're good sweetie, just go and see what else he wants and I will be here waiting for you."

Chapter 10

Cookie

Jumping into my car, I tried to get to the shop as fast as I could. So much was going through my mind, and I started to think about my husband and my best friend. I know I have always been a good wife to him and a good friend to her.

Grabbing my phone and going to my Apple Music station, I pulled up Kelly Price's "Friend of Mine". I had that shit blasting and singing as loud as I could. This song was on point with my life right now. The tears started pouring down my face and anger started to surface.

Thicker...than blood, wherever there was me, there was you. Hmm, my all was your all. But that wasn't enough for yoooou, you had to seeee, and tried to walk a mile in my shoooes...

Singing to the top of my lungs, I made a sharp turn and almost ran into a little old lady walking across the street.

I wasn't really fucked up over Brandon. I shot his ass off the strength of me seeing him eat her pussy better than he ever ate mine. I shot her because she was my sister. Watching her enjoy my husband like that had me heated. How can your best friend do something like that to you? It makes you question everything about them. Like bitch, you were never really my friend. It ain't shit a nigga can say to you that would make you do some shit like that. The first time it was with my first love in high school, and I forgave her for that. Now it's my husband, and I was not about to let her do it to the next man.

So much was running through my head right now, I honestly can't believe I just had to kill my friend. Tears started to run down my face as I reflected back on the first time we met.

I walked into my first-period class after being transferred from another school. She was sitting in the back of the room, and it was an empty desk right next to her. Taking a seat and once Mrs. McCloud started talking, I realized my ass didn't go to my locker before class and everything was in there. I asked her for paper and a pen to take notes. She gave me a big ass Five Star notebook and two packs of pens.

"Thanks," I quietly said so I wouldn't disturb the class. She just gave me a head nod indicating it was cool.

After first period, we walked to our next class and turned out her ass was in that class too. We talked more in this one and compared our schedule to see they put us in all of the same classes. What a coincidence. From that day forward, we were two peas in a pod. She would call me in the mornings asking what I was wearing to school, and I get there to see she's wearing the same colors and had us walking around like the Doublemint twins. I introduced her to my mom one day when she came over after school. The look on my mom's face was strange for some reason, but she still played nice.

Noelle left after we finished our homework, and my mom walked in my room and said, "London, you better watch her, it's something about that lil' girl I don't like." They always say your man and your mom will always tell you who your friends are. If either one of them says, "that's not your friend" you better listen. I didn't listen to my mom, Noelle became my best friend, someone I felt like I could trust with anything, including my life.

***

"FIGHT! FIGHT! FIGHT! FIGHT!" was all I heard as I walked out of the bathroom in between my next class.

I pushed through the crowd and saw it was two girls getting the best of Noelle. I jumped in quick, fucking the biggest one up. I may be pretty, but these hands are deadly. Boxing was something I did during the summers when I was out of school. After reading a ton of books all day, I would go over to my dad's gym and have a session with one of the guys. I beat that bitch until she was begging for me to stop. The principle came and broke it up, and all of our asses got suspended for a week, but they gave my ass two. Ever since she saw how hard I was rocking with her, you couldn't pull our ass apart. That was my bitch, my sister, my bestie!

Finally, I pulled up to the shop. "Get yourself together Cookie!" I spoke aloud to myself, pulling my visor down so I could clean my face before I walked into this building. I had dried up tears running all down my face.

Parking next to Jonquill's truck, I quickly jumped out and made my way inside.

"What's going on guys?" I questioned, as soon as I stepped in. Noticing the look on everyone face, things did not look good.

"Read this!" Jon B requested, handing me his phone.

B: I HAVE DECIDED TO LET EVERYTHING GO THERE. SHIT WASN'T WORKING OUT AND I NEEDED TO GET AWAY. I HAVE FOUND SOMEONE ELSE AND I DIDN'T HAVE THE GUTS TO TELL COOKIE BECAUSE I KNOW HOW IT WOULD HURT HER IF SHE FOUND OUT I WAS NOW WITH HER ONE AND ONLY BEST FRIEND. EVERYTHING IS HERS— THE HOUSE AND THE SHOPS— SO YOU HAVE TO ASK HER WHAT SHE CHOOSES TO DO WITH IT. I'M SORRY IT HAD TO END LIKE THIS, BUT I CAN'T GO ON LIVING THIS LIE.

-B

"What type of fuck shit is this?" I yelled out as tears started to fill up in my eyes.

Jon B pulled me into his chest where I just let it all out. I wasn't crying because of the text; I was crying because of the overall bullshit. Last night had me going crazy, and even though I fucked both of them up, I'm still fucking hurt by that bullshit. Chase came to my rescue though, and I was happy. He didn't ask any questions; he just hopped on the next flight out.

"I know this may not be a good time for this type of question Cookie, but with him being gone, what do you plan on doing with the shop? He had this one, and he was finalizing things with the other one across town," Jonquill asked. Shit, I don't give two flying fucks what they do with this bullshit. I have no use for it at all.

"Shit, y'all can flip a coin and choose which shop y'all want to run. If he left me to go be with a bitch, then I don't want any parts of his business. Heads Jon B gets Klean Kuts and tails Jonquill gets the other shop. Have at it!" I proceeded to walk out the door.

Grabbing my phone out of my back pocket, I continued to call up British. She hasn't answered since she left the shop last night and I am starting to worry about her.

***

One month later

Once I got everything squared away with the police and the shops, I decided to stick around a little while longer, just so things would not look suspicious with me just up and leaving all of a sudden. Chase was still coming to see me and blowing my mind each time he came until I finally decided to make that move with him. No one was asking about Brandon anymore, and if they did, I told them that I wanted to move past it all and start over fresh, so once I finally did move, they would already know why.

Today is moving day, and it was time to leave. I had Jon B send me the text Brandon sent his phone that night and show it to my cousin who is a police officer. The last thing I wanted was his family to do was file a missing person report, and they start questioning me. I wanted the police to already know his ass ran off and he is not missing, just in case his family started asking questions later.

"Are you sure you are ready to make this move?" Chase asked as we loaded the last of my things into the moving truck and we headed to the airport.

"Yes, we are good. I'm excited to get to Miami to enjoy my new life. I'm happy to start working for a new school. I hope the kids aren't as bad there as they are here," I tried to sound excited as possible. The truth is I could give a damn about those kids at that moment; I was still trying to get myself back together.

"You don't have to go back if you don't want to. I make enough for the both of us."

"I have money myself; I just like being with kids. Since I don't have any of my own, I like helping the ones that I can. "Each one teach one" is my motto, and I don't see myself doing anything but that right now."

"That's cool; I hope you will be ok at home alone. I have a business meeting in New York tomorrow, so I will be gone a day or two. I'm sure you know how to handle your own."

"I'll be just fine, you already know me. I'm about that life for real if anybody come fucking with me." We laugh together as we boarded the plane.

I tried to make one last phone call to British before I left. She must be on an all-night sex trip because that's the only reason she wouldn't answer or return my calls. We loaded the plane first class, and I knocked back as many drinks as I could to get the thoughts of my husband and my best friend lifeless body lying there. Even though it has been a month, I still have dreams about it.

***

"Of course you already know where everything is since you were just here. Make yourself at home; this is your new place. Anything you want to change you can or throw out you are more than welcome to. I want to make this transition as smooth as possible for you," Chase stated, walking me upstairs to our bedroom.

"Thank you. I'm sure there is something in this big ass house that I can toss the hell out or burn to make it more feminine."

"Do whatever you choose, as long as you keep my side of the bed warm for me," Chase stated as he started grabbing up his things to get ready for his business trip.

Chapter 11

British

I've been in this bed for four days now. I have watched the sun rise and set like clockwork. As soon as night falls, Tank always come his ass in the house, let me shower, use the bathroom and fuck the shit out of me. It's like he was using me for his own personal little sex slave. I know I have done some pretty fucked up things, but I still do not think I deserve to be treated like this.

The sun was starting to set, and I knew it was only a matter of minutes before he came in. Moments later the door swung open, and he walked in, but this time he only untied me and walked back out the house. *What type of bullshit is this?* I thought to myself. I had gotten used to fucking at the same time every day so shit my pussy was anticipating that good dick I was about to receive.

I managed to stumble out of bed, stretching my body a few good times since I have been laying awhile. Making my way to the door, I saw that he was sitting outside in the car waiting on me to come out. Once he saw me walking outside, he quickly jumped out of the car and helped me inside. We drove off without a word said to each other. I couldn't even get an I'm sorry, yo pussy was too good to let you slip away or nothing. He just drove away and headed towards my house. Once we pulled up, he came around, lifted me out of the car, and carried me to the house.

"So you're not going to say anything to me? I think I deserve to know what all of that was about," I questioned. He unlocked my door and walked me into the bedroom, still not saying any words.

Placing me on the bed, he walked into my bathroom and started running bath water. He lifted me from the bed bridal style and carried me into the bathroom. This nigga must be crazy as the fuck cause he won't say a damn thing to me.

"Look just put me down! I can do this shit myself. Since you can't explain yourself, you can get the fuck out of my house. Yo ass had me confined to a bed for days using me for sex, and now you come yo ass in my house and ain't said a damn thing, acting like shit sweet!" I spat, pushing him out of my bathroom.

He started undressing himself, made his way to my tub, and got in. My eyes roamed all over his body, and my pussy started to get wet just looking at him; the water was barely covering his dick up.

"Get in!" he demanded. I stood there with my arms folded, and I did not move. "I said get in!" his deep-voiced boomed throughout my bathroom, causing me to jump. I quickly undressed myself and stepped in. He laid my head back on his chest and kissed me on my neck.

"I'm sorry," he whispered in my ear and started washing my body up.

***

"Ooooh shit, Tank. Fuck!" I moaned out with much pleasure.

Tank stayed the night with me and woke me up to breakfast and head. He apologized for holding me fucking hostage for days. I know you guys are probably thinking I'm the crazy one for being cool and calm with his ass, but it's just something about his crazy ass that I am really feeling. Not to mention he did do this pussy right when he had me tied up.

"Make that pussy cum for me," he whispered gently flicking his tongue around my clit and softly sucked on my pussy lips. Before I knew it, I was cumin' all over his chin.

"Hmmm!" he moaned out. "This is my pussy; I don't want nobody else in my pussy." He started back eating my pussy like the true beast he is. He came up and then all of a sudden he turned into this other person. He flipped me over by my leg, with one hand and pushed himself inside of me. Wrapping my legs around him, he picked me up off the bed and started bouncing me hard on his dick.

"Shit this pussy is tight as fuck," he managed to get out in between kisses.

"Get on the bed," he demanded. I jumped on the bed, and he came up behind me.

Pushing the top half of my body off the bed, he now had me in an upside down push up position. My hands were on the floor, and he was on his knees on the bed, he had my legs up like I was a damn wheel barrel and was fucking me like crazy. I have never been in that type of position before and honestly only a crazy person would think of some shit like this.

I was holding on to the carpet for dear life, all while my blood was rushing to my head. I wanted to scream out let me up, but I also wanted to get this nut first.

***

One month later

"Bitch, where have you been? I've been blowing your fucking phone up for over a month. I was really worried about you. Yo mama didn't even know where you were," Cookie blurted out as soon as I answered the phone.

"Girl, I told you about the man I met that same night you met your mystery man. I want to say he kidnapped my ass but I'm a grown ass woman so what is it, Woman-napped? Yea, that nigga woman-napped my ass and fucked the shit out of me for four days, well three days. On the fourth day, he let my ass go like didn't shit happen, brought me to my house, took a bath with me, and woke me up to some bomb ass head and mind blowing dick."

"You are fucking crazy yo damn self if you are actually ok with that bullshit. I'm sure his crazy ass didn't use a condom. Yo ass gone wake up pregnant by his crazy ass."

"Wake up pregnant! L-O-L haha real funny. I'm on that good birth control."

"The birth control that yo ass ain't been on since he had your ass locked up."

Cookie, talking crazy, I know how to handle my shit. He may be crazy as Dominic Demonte from the book series *Married to the Mob* by Mz Lady P that I was reading on my Kindle. That nigga was a nut case for real but definitely one of my book baes.

"Whatever girl, I know I'm good, ain't no babies coming this way. Anyway, what you on, you got your little situation handled?

"Yea everything is good I'm out in Miami, You should fly out tomorrow to visit me. Chase is going out of town for a few days, and this house is too fucking big to be here alone."

"Bitch fuck that, I will fly out tonight. You know I already halfway like it here. Fuck around and make me come with all my shit and say fuck all of this bullshit."

"That's cool just let me know if you fly out tonight or tomorrow so I can pick you up."

We got off the phone, and I immediately stated the packing majority of my shit. I already know Cookie ass about to have me turning the fuck up in Miami.

***

"Girl this shit is fucking fly as hell," I stated, while she took me on a tour of this big ass house,

"British, you are so fucking country. Stop acting like you ain't never seen a big ass house before. On top of that, Chase is in bed asleep. He has an early flight to New York in the morning him and his brother."

"Brother? Let me find out I'm about to have me a new man." I laughed but deep down I was dead ass serious. Tank ain't my nigga so I'm sure I can dibble and dabble with new meat here and there.

She took me on a tour of the rest of the house and outside to the guesthouse where I will be staying. Everything was so damn nice. I'm glad it didn't take her no time to move on. If I found out my nigga was fucking my friend, I would nut the fuck up and fall into a deep long dark depression. Losing my mind would be only the half of it. But shit, Cookie bossed the fuck up and moved on to bigger and better things. On top of Chase being fine as hell, this nigga has money, and it shows.

"Here pop this open, let's have a drink because I'm in desperate need of one," Cookie announced, passing me the bottle of Rose'. I could look and tell she was about to go in from the look on her face.

"What's up, Cookie? What's on your mind?"

"I'm really fucked up inside, British. I'm sitting here pretending like I'm good with everything, and I am not. That shit really hurt me that no one cared about how London would feel if she found out they were fucking. They were just worried about getting their next nut out. I don't understaaaand!" she yelled out and threw a drink back and poured herself another one.

"Why me though, B? That was my husband. He was supposed to love me through all of the bullshit, through all of the pain that he inflicted on me, might I add. I was a good wife and friend; I didn't deserve this. Then the bitch was laid up in my fucking house in that funky ass Chanel No 9 perfume. Where was the fucking respect for me? That bitch could have taken her ass to a Motel 6, anywhere but my fucking bed."

I moved closer to her and wrapped my arms around her. This was not the moment for me to say I told you so. At this moment, she just needed someone to listen.

Usually, I never listen. I am always so quick to pop off at the mouth and speak on something that I don't know. I've never been in her shoes, so I can't say stop crying, or things would be good. I would be lying if I did.

"It's ok Cookie, just let it out!" I continued to rub her back, and she continued to let out her frustration.

"All I ever wanted was for someone to love me and only me. Not tolerate me and love someone else. Hell, I could tell by the way he was eating her pussy that he loved her."

"Let me love you," Chase appeared out of nowhere in the doorway of the guesthouse and scared the shit out of the both of us. "I want to be that man that you can call on at any hour. I want to be your best friend. No disrespect to British, but when things go good in your life, I want you to call me. When things are fucked up, I want you to call me. I want to be that knight in Gucci armor that comes to your rescue." He stepped into her space, and I quickly stepped out of the way. "Just trust me is all that I ask of you. One thing you will never have to worry about is me cheating or lying to you about anything."

By this time, she is looking at him with tears flowing out of her eyes. I don't know if they were happy tears or if the bitch was still sad about catching two bodies. I turned and walked back up to the house and gave them their space.

"Tank?" I blurted out when I stepped on the porch and saw him sitting there smoking a blunt. "What are you doing here?"

"I should be asking you the same question." He jumped up in my space. "I KNOW YOU'RE NOT FUCKING MY BROTHER?"

"Your brother? Chase! Hell no, that nigga fucking my cousin, she's in the guesthouse with him right now. They needed some privacy, so I decided to walk back up here to the house."

"Let's go have some privacy of our own." He picked me up, carried me back off the porch, and pulled down the bed of his truck.

"You call this privacy?" I asked.

"Hell yea cause when they hear yo ass scream they won't get any closer so that sound like a bunch of privacy to me. Plus it's about to rain, and I've always wanted to fuck in the rain."

Yea, this nigga is all types of crazy, but since I am horny, I'm with the shit right with his ass. He started snatching off my yoga pants and went face first into this pussy. I'm glad I just washed it before my flight cause he didn't waste no time.

Chapter 12

Cookie

I didn't expect for Chase to walk in and hear my conversation with British. I wanted him to think I was over the entire situation. He coming in and saying all that good shit to me had a bitch's heart melting. Chase is a big solid dude, so you wouldn't expect his ass to be so soft like that. When I woke up this morning, he left money on the dresser and a note that said.

You were great last night, so I had to pay you for your services.
This should be enough for you to enjoy yourself until I come home.
I know this nigga didn't! I said to myself.
Flip paper over...
It was a joke; you know you are more than just a piece of ass to me. I did leave money though, and that's for you to enjoy yourself with until I come back. Once I do, it's all about you. I want to learn more about you. What makes you laugh? What makes you cry? What position do you have to be in to get knocked up?
Enjoy yourself! See you when I come home.
-Yo NEW Daddy

I rolled around in the bed for a minute thinking of how this man is already showing me he is different from my husband.

Opening up the curtains in the bedroom, I looked outside and saw British was already at the pool with her IPad. I walked into the bathroom and did my morning routine before I grabbed my iPad and headed outside with her. My skin was already popping, but this sun is about to give me a nice little tan.

"Bout time you woke up, hoe!" British stated, as soon as I made my way out the back door.

"Girl hush, I had a long ass night."

"Me too!" I couldn't help but notice the hickeys she had on her stomach and at the top of her cleavage.

"Now, I know you ain't been here that long to find a nigga that fast. You didn't even try to hide the hickeys all over your body."

"I could have, but why? The last time I checked, I was grown as hell, and my body is just that, my body. Surprisingly, Tank was already here when I came from around back. I didn't know he was Chase's brother. Why didn't you tell me?"

"If I had known you knew him, I would have. You never mentioned his name before."

"Girl, that's the nigga I told you about, who had my ass tied up for three fucking days."

I met Tank when I came here the first time, but he didn't stay long because he was catching the next flight back out. Little did I know it was to be with my cousin.

"My bad, I had no idea, Oh well! What are you over there reading? It's got yo ass out here early."

"This new book by this author Trenae' called *You Gon' Pay Me With Tears*. I've been out here so long I had time to finish up *Where I Want To Be* by Manda P.

"Oh girl that one is not her newest one, trust me, I follow her ass on every social media site she has. *Wishing He Was My Savage*, is her newest one. Anyway, how long are you gone be out here? Chase left me some money this morning, so I'm about to go and see what Miami has for me."

"Not long, just let me finish a few more chapters. Tank left me money on the dresser like a $2 hoe too." We laughed together and started back reading our books and watched as the pool guy came around and started cleaning the leaves out of the pool.

***

We jumped into my car that Chase had transported here and headed straight to the boutiques. I don't need shit because of the first time I came. I still had all of the shit in the room waiting on me to come back, but you know a girl can never have too many clothes and shoes, so I'm sure it's something that will catch my eye.

BUZZ BUZZ

The buzzing of my phone started going off back to back like it was a damn amber alert going off.

J: Why didn't we tell him about us?

J: You know I hated seeing someone else come to your rescue.

J: You already knew you could have called on me first before anything.

J: I'm not over you.

J: I waited on you to leave Brandon, now it looks like I have to get rid of this one myself.

J: Friend or not, that nigga gotta go.

"Girl who is that blowing you up like that?" British asked.

"My damn ex. He's on some more shit right now, and if I respond he may think he actually has a chance in hell with me but nah, I'ma ride this one out. Eventually, he will get tired and leave my ass alone.

We pulled up to this boutique called Purple Reign. I heard Trenae' mention it in her book, but I didn't know it was an actual place.

Stepping inside of the store my eyes landed on this cute black catsuit with some thigh-high boots to match. I may just be cat woman when Chase makes it back home.

"What you see?" I asked British. She was walking around with this ugly ass mug on her face.

"Not shit! This big ass store and I don't see anything for me, not even a fucking pair of leggings."

"I guess girl. Let's go. we will try somewhere else."

I paid for my stuff, and we left out of the store. British was tripping. That store was full up nice shit. Her ass just got that big donkey ass and can't get shit over it. The only jeans that fit her ass that's made for bitches with a small waist line is Fashion Nova.

We walked down the boulevard going in and out of shops. I started to get tired and hungry. I saw a food truck across the street, and I've always wanted to try one. On our way across the street, I took out my phone to check on Chase. He left out this morning, but I haven't heard from him since. He was supposed to call and let me know that he made it safely.

The phone had ringed a few times before I heard someone pick up.

"Tell her to stop calling you!" Then the phone quickly hung up.

I must have called his phone until mine started to go dead. This is the shit I'm talking about. This nigga just said plain and clear yesterday that he would never lie or cheat. Here he is doing them both. *"Tell her to stop calling you!"* What type of shit is that to say? Chase ain't been my man a full 60 seconds yet and this nigga already wit' the shit.

I'm trying my best to be patient and wait on this man to return my phone call or even just come home. My body was burning with anticipation. I had so much on my mind, and he really needs to get here before I get ghost on his ass. I watched British get all excited when her phone started going off. It's nobody but Tank ass calling her and I'm sitting here still waiting on Chase just to reply back to my text. Once I heard her about to end the call, I got up and snatched her phone out of her hand.

"Where the fuck is Chase?" I spat through the receiver.

"Look Cookie! I don't know if you heard about me or not, but I'm the brother that's always with the shit. What you won't do is yell at me.

If you want to know where Chase is, you need to call Chase's phone. Now, I hate being interrupted so if you don't mind put British back on the phone and quickly."

"Tank, I don't know who you thought this was, but I'm the woman that's with the shit too. Your little threat was far from scary, and honestly, it made me laugh on the inside. That shit might scare British, but my Miniature Poodle bark is bigger than yours is. Now I'ma ask you again, where the fuck is Chase?"

All I heard was the dial tone that lil' nigga hung up on me. But it's cool, he still heard what the fuck I said, and I'm sure he will get the message to Chase. I told y'all that soft bitch that once lived in me is dead, and this one right here could give a fuck about if he like being interrupted or not. I don't like bitches hanging up on me, but he did.

***

Once we made it back home, I went into the room and started packing my clothes up. Chase had another thing coming if he thought I was about to just sit here wondering and worrying about him. Not knowing if he is with a bitch or not, that lil' shit she said does not sit well with me.

Why can't men ever do right? We sit here and give their asses fair fucking warnings, and they continuously do what we beg them not to do. We tell them not to drink out the carton, and they do, don't forget to let the toilet seat down, and they do. Don't smack my ass that hard, and they do. Niggas! I couldn't do anything but shake my head at the thought of him.

The more and more I thought about him being away, it took me back to him trying to explain his line of work. I never got a full answer from his ass.

"British, come here for a second!" I called out for her; she was in the next bedroom.

"What's good?"

"Did Tank ever tell you what he and Chase do as far as to make their money?"

"He said he runs a damn dating service or some shit."

"Bitch, a dating service? Shut the fuck up!" I replied with a loud ass laugh. This shit cannot be real. This man wants to be the next head nigga in charge for *BlackPeopleMeet.com*

Walking into his office, I decided to do a little snooping. I knew that lil' job had to be a front. After going to many drawers, I finally found a key to a locked cabinet. As soon as I opened it, pictures of naked women and video tapes fell out. My heart sunk into my stomach.

Covering my mouth I started going through the pictures, most of them had numbers on the back of them— *Candy 103,098 Duchess 75K Tonya 300K.* This shit had my mind racing and sick to my stomach seeing how all of these hoes was busting that pussy open on these pictures. I didn't even bother watching the video. I know it's probably some shit on there that I do not want to see.

BUZZ BUZZ

Chase: I know you are angry, but we will talk when I come home. See you later on this evening

Throwing my phone to the side, I didn't even bother to reply to that bullshit. It took his ass too long to reply to me.

"What's this?" British asked, looking at all of the pictures scattered over the floor.

"I have no idea, but I'm going to find out. I found this directory with a lot of women names in it. How about we throw the guys a surprise party?" I'm sure he probably fucked half of these women since they were laid up willingly posing for pictures and shit."

Passing half of the list to British to call and I called the others. He gone have to explain this shit to me, today.

***

"Surpriiiisssse!!!" we all jumped up yelling as soon as the guys walked in. The look on Chase's face was priceless. I grabbed my bag and walked out the door. He can have each and every one of those ladies. No longer will I tolerate lies.

The girls had music blasting, popping bottles, and throwing money on the strippers I hired.

"Where do you think you are going?" Chase snatched me back by the arm and had this furious look in his eyes.

"I'm going home because you are just like my fucking husband— a damn liar! Tell your lil' bitch that answered the phone she can have your lying ass. I'm good on you, Chase." I snatched my arm back and tried to rush to my car.

The next thing I know I was being lifted off the ground and put in the front seat of his car by Tank. Chase jumped in the driver seat and drove off before I got a chance to jump the fuck out.

"Chase, I am only going to say this once, pull this car over so I can take my ass home. You have a house full of women, so you don't need me."

"You called them, not me! Those women are not my women, well they are but not in that way. They just work for me. I was going to tell you when the time was right."

"Work for you like what, Chase? Are you a pimp or something?"

"Sorta."

That was definitely not what I wanted to hear. After we had driven around a while, he explained the business to me. He told me how it was passed down to him and his brother Tank. I just wish he had been honest from the beginning.

"I understand all that but what about the bitch that answered your phone? What was all that?"

"That was my assistant Charmaine; she was just bullshitin'. She knows we are not on that level at all. I haven't fucked with anyone heavy since my wife got killed. It's females that I fucked with, but not on the level I'm on with you. Cookie, when I said I wanted to be there for you and love you, all that was real. What I do for a living is the only thing I kept from you. From here on out there won't be any secrets between us. That goes for you as well. Don't keep nothing from me."

We started heading towards the house, and I was already feeling bad about inviting all of those women there for a party. Good thing he has a maid because I know that place is fucked up.

***

"Damn, who cleaned up everything?" I stated as I looked around and saw no one but British and Tank in sight.

"Tank's ass made them clean up and kicked them out."

"If they wanted to keep their jobs they had to get the fuck out of here. Boss man left so they needed to leave too," Tank replied. I can already see this nigga have some real life issues on his hands.

Chapter 13

Tremaine "Tank" Williams

"Are you still having those nightmares, Mr. Williams?" my psychiatrist asked as I laid across her couch.

I have been seeing Dr. Townsend ever since I got out of the military. Seeing all of those bodies blown in half, kids being killed because they are strapped with bombs and even seeing my best friend get killed, had me completely traumatized. I tried my best to save him when they snatched him up.

Laying low with a pile of leaves over my body, I watched as they threw him in the back of the truck and drove off. I couldn't yell out to him because they would have gotten me too. That phrase *I am my brother's keeper* didn't apply to me since I let my brother get killed. Shit, I may as well had been the one who beheaded him since I am the one who allowed it to happen. Till this day I still have nightmares of them showing him sitting there waiting to get his head cut off on national television.

Having PTSD —Post-Traumatic Stress Disorder— has me on a mental, emotional roller coaster. No one really understands what I have been through unless they have dealt with it themselves. I became numb to a lot of things. Thoughts of someone loving me went away a long time ago. No one would want to be with a man like me. I'm too much to handle, period.

That shit I pulled with British, that wasn't me. She is beautiful in every way. The most beautiful woman I have ever seen besides my mother, actually. All I really wanted to do was keep her to myself, so she wouldn't think about leaving me how everyone else has.

Once I told my sister Cassie what I had done, she talked me into letting her go. She said if British was going to love me she would do it on her own. So, against my better judgment, I let her go. Once I saw her here in Miami, I knew then she was meant to be with me. Why else would she fly here? She tried to pull that stunt like she didn't know I was Chase brother. The truth is, she really came back so I could tie her ass up again and this time make her have my seeds.

"Tremaine... Tremaine!" I could hear Dr. Townsend calling out to me, but my body was stuck. I opened my mouth, but the words wouldn't come out. She started shaking my body back and forth to get me out of the trance I was in.

"Tremaine!" she called out one more time

"WHAT!" I yelled, causing her to jump back.

"Have you been taking your medication properly?"

"Yes," I lied. I haven't touched a pill since I ran out three weeks ago, but she didn't need to know all of that.

"How have you been feeling lately?"

Honestly, I have been having these reoccurring nightmares of this kid walking up to me with bombs on him. Thoughts of suicide crossed my mind several times in a day. I just want to be left alone, and that is the only way I know no one would be able to bother me. My heart is cold now, and I don't know how to make it right again.

"Yes, I take my medication faithfully every morning. I don't even think I need too many more of these private sessions. I would much rather stay at home and deal with this shit as it comes. I'm just paying you money to listen to me talk. I'm pretty sure any crackhead off the street can do that and charge me way less."

The only thing that helps me cope with what happened is when I kill someone. It may sound weird, but it helps me get the frustration out of not being able to kill the people who killed my friend.

"You call the shots Tremaine remember I'm always here if you need me," she said and walked me out of her office.

***

Sitting on my back porch, I started preparing for my next assignment.

One of my guys introduced me to the man that's head of this crime mob. We have never met face to face; I only talk through one of his head workers. He hired me to get rid of a couple of people for him—249 people to be exact. My next mark is this guy named, Valentin. He flaked on boss man with some guns when they did their last trade. He usually hides out at this underground club, and it's invite only, but me and my AR-15 don't need an invite.

Stepping into my bedroom, I see candles lit all around my room. I pulled my Glock from my back and moved around the room slowly. Hearing the sound of water in my bathroom, I pushed the door open.

"Trina, what the fuck are you doing in my house?" I yelled at the sight of seeing my ex lying in my bathtub.

Trina and I broke up after I came back from the military. She is one of the ones who couldn't handle my PTSD and left my ass. Now she's sitting here asshole naked in my tub about to set my room on fire with all these funky ass candles and shit.

"I missed you Tank, and I know you missed me too. I'm sorry for walking out on you when you needed me the most. Let me make it up to you." She stepped out of the tub, and I watched as the suds started to roll down her body. My dick started getting hard at the sight of her.

Dropping down to her knees, she pulled my dick out and took it inch by inch into her mouth. Her mouth was wetter than her pussy has ever been. She started to deep throat my dick making my damn eyes roll to the back of my head, and my toes curl.

"Let it out baby," she whispered. I felt myself getting ready to drop my seeds off in her mouth.

POW! POW!

Trina's body fell to the floor, and her brains went all over my walls. I tried to move fast to get my gun from the side of the sink, then I saw her.

"Bitch, you could have blown my fucking dick off."

"Nigga, if yo dick is up there by her damn brain, then you need to go see a specialist for that retarded ass dick." She turned and walked out of the bathroom then almost immediately spun back around on her heels.

"You thought I was going to let you nut in another bitch, whether it was her pussy or her mouth. That shit was not gonna happen. You tied me up for four days, fucked the shit out of me, and made love to my pussy with your mouth the next morning. So if you ask me, that means we go together. Now, let me come over here again and another bitch is sucking my dick then she's gone get the same treatment. Clean this shit up and come give me some dick and wash that hoe's spit off first."

British came in and bossed up on me, and that shit really turned me on. I have never had a woman to handle me like that before. Fuck cleaning Trina up; I need that pussy now.

I reached in the tub and let out the water that Trina was sitting in and turned the shower water on. Damn waiting till the water was all drained out I needed to soap this dick up real quick so I jumped right in.

Washing my body up a few times, I grabbed my towel and went right into my bedroom. British was laying on the bed looking like a snack, and I couldn't wait to feast on her.

***

After about an hour of hard fucking, she started running her some bath water and watched as I cleaned Trina and her brains off my walls.

"Once I dump her, I have to step out and handle some business real quick. You sit tight and keep that pussy wet for me until I make it back home."

"Yes, big daddy! I will be right here" She blew me a kiss as I walked out of the door.

I pulled out the most expensive suit I could find in my closet, my all black Brioni Colosseo suit with some black loafers. The is not an ordinary nightclub, so I had to walk in like I was dressed to kill, LITERALLY!

I grabbed the keys to my Maserati and did the dash to the club.

"What's up T," my guy Israel said as I threw the valet attendant next to him my keys. He is the bouncer here so getting into the club would be easy, getting to Valentin would be the hard part. He always has double tight security.

"Shit, keep my shit running you know I will be in and out."

I walked into my private VIP section and waited for the right time to get the job done.

ME: NOW!

As soon as I sent that text, a fight broke out with his security to create a distraction. They closed the curtains where he was sitting, and I slipped right in the side.

"What the fuck are you doing in my section?" Valentin blurted, as soon as he saw me slide in.

"The next time you wanna get over on somebody, DON'T!" before he got a chance to say anything else, I sent two through the side of his neck and left back out the curtains.

Chapter 14

Cookie

Resting my head on his chest, I noticed how his heartbeat matched mine. That part alone had chills going through my body. I used to listen to Brandon's heart, and I swear that bitch would stop beating every now and then. He must have been a real life devil on earth.

It's been a month since I just got up and moved away and no one from his family has even tried to contact me. I thought I would be hurt still, but Chase has given me every reason in the world to forget about my past and look forward to my future with him.

British is supposed to come over in a little while. I wanted her to ride with me to pick something up. This has been bothering me for a few days now.

BUZZ BUZZ

J: See you soon.

Shit, I thought if I ignored all of his messages that he would just get the hint that I do not want his ass anymore. Justin is old news, and I'm not trying to mess my relationship up for him. He had his chance so now it's time for a real man to teach me how to love.

"I will be back in a few, babe," I said when I saw British pull up outside.

"Let me find out I got the wrong brother. There ain't no way he let yo non-driving ass get behind the wheels of his Maserati. You stole it, huh? Tell the truth," I joked, making us both laugh and she sped off to the nearest Walmart.

"What do you need to come here for?"

"A damn pregnancy test, my cycle is three days late."

"Grab me one too shit. I'm not getting out. This man car probably cost more than Walmart."

I ran inside of the store and grabbed four test, two for me and two for her. Once I checked out, I hauled ass back to the car.

***

"What does yours say?"

"Bitch, it says I need bottles, wipes, and diapers!" British yelled out making me laugh at her crazy ass. I told her ass he was gone get her knocked up.

"You?" she asked.

"It says I need to start storing breast milk and catching up on my sleep now cause my ass gone be up all night."

In a way, I was happy as hell but also nervous like I just lost my virginity for the first time. I know Chase will be a great father; I just have to find faith in myself to know I will be a great mother.

My family has not always been close. Love is something that was hard to find in the blood that runs through my family veins. I refuse to be anything like my mother. Being the only child, I damn near raised myself. My father was a hustler, so he was rarely home. My mom did her own thing; where she was at was always a mystery to me.

When I graduated, I moved off to college and vowed to be more than them. I got my Masters in Education and moved back home to work at my old high school.

"Hey! Lucinda made lunch. You wanna come in the house and get you some before it gets cold. I'm telling you she makes the best chicken club sandwich you have ever tasted," Chase's voice startled me as he stepped into the guesthouse where British and I were.

"Babe, I will be up there in a minute; that shit does sound good as hell."

"What's that behind your back?" I tried hiding the test from him because I wanted to wait till later to tell him.

"A pregnancy test, that bitch is full of baby and so am I. So I guess you are a new father and a new uncle. Now let me go upstairs and grab me one of Lucinda sandwiches. Oh, Lucccccindaaa!" British blurted out in a Spanish accent and left out the door.

At that moment, I really wanted to beat her ass and bust her head to the white meat. British means well but sometimes her mouth gets her into a lot of shit.

Chase started walking up on me and reached his hand out. I put the test in his hand and studied his face.

"You might want to dig up B, and let him know he's got a shorty on the way." He dropped the test and walked out the door.

My heart sunk into my stomach and tears ran down my face faster than roaches run out the kitchen when you turn the lights on. I covered my face up with my hands and cried. I couldn't believe he said that to me. Brandon and I haven't had sex in months, so I know this is Chase baby. Him denying it, made me go from hurt to furious real quick. Jumping up off the couch, I rushed up to the house. Chase had another thing coming if he thought I was just gone let him fuck me like this.

British's bitch ass was sitting at the kitchen table stuffing her face with sandwiches and chips. I popped her ass in the back of the head and ran upstairs.

Swinging the bedroom door open, I was met with candles, pink and blue balloons, and Chase down on one knee with a big ass ring.

"London "Cookie" Bridges, from the moment I saw you I knew then that you were going to be my wife. It was the way my heart raced as I approached you. When I spoke my first words to you, I felt like I was breathing new air again. Cookie, I need you to continue to be my air forever. I'm sorry about what I did in the guesthouse. I already knew you were pregnant. I texted British when you left out the house so fast.

Three days late, right? I can't wait to be a father to my twins. Cookie, please say YES!" I was standing there in total shock.

Here I was ready to fuck him up how I did Brandon and Noelle bitch asses. I wanted to say yes, but I was truly scared— scared for my heart. Granted Chase is a good man, but at the end of the day, he is a man. It's plenty of Noelle's walking around Miami, and just like Brandon, it took nothing for him to start fucking her brains out.

"Cookie!" Chase called out, pulling me from my thoughts. "Trust me; I am not Brandon, I will never do what he did to you. You are more than enough woman for me, and no one else can ever come and take my attention away from you. I love you, and I know you love me." I hesitated for a second before giving him my answer.

"Yes Chase, I will marry you. But first, that lil' bitch that said 'Tell her to stop calling you' has to go. I don't care what you say, but that bitch wanna fuck. I promised myself that I would never let a bitch get 12-inch dick length to my man before I put them paws on her ass. Whatever her job was, it's mine now!"

"Done, whatever you want, you got it! Just know when that stomach starts meeting people before you, you gone have to sit yo ass down."
***

Chase arranged a meeting with all of the girls and me. I only met a few of them that day at the party, so it was only fair for them to officially meet the new head bitch in charge. The part I'm about to love the most out of this is telling, Ms. "I wanna play games on the phone" Charmaine, that we no longer need her services. She is not allowed anywhere near the girls or Chase, and all contact must cease today or she gone have to deal with me.

I made sure to put my big girl Boss outfit on. It was this Cream pantsuit that fitted around my ass and flared out at the bottom. I wore this one button blazer with no shirt or bra underneath, Thanks to Brandon on that boob job our first year of marriage. Of course, I had to throw on my Christian Louboutin to set my fit off.
***

"Good afternoon ladies, those of you may or may not know who I am. I am Cookie, Chase's FIANCÉE" I made sure I put emphasis on that word for the hoes that slick wants my man. "There will be a few changes around here. For starters, Chase is no longer your boss, I am! Whatever you were calling him for, you will now call me. If and only if I think what you need is out of my control in some way then, I will get the message over to him. When you make trips, you are to report to me as soon as you get there and when you leave.

Each girl will have this right here inserted in their wrist." I held up a tiny tracking device. "This is only so if a nigga gets wrong and yo ass comes up missing, then I can find you. It does have an alert button on it that will send a silent signal indicating you need help and it also enables me to hear what's going on around you.

Now, I'm not saying you will ever be in this type of danger because most of you have regulars that you deal with. Just in case that nigga is off his meds one day and try some slick shit, know that Mrs. Cookie got you and I will be there to wreck shit."

"Where was this shit when Brandon crazy ass kept attacking me? I had to wait till that nigga left out the room to call Chase," one of the ladies said.

"Excuse me, who did you say?"

"Brandon, he has been my regular for over two years now and come to think of it I haven't heard from his ass in over a month. He and that weak ass wife of his must have gotten back together. That's the only time he does not come and blow stacks on me."

My heart started beating rapidly. I didn't know if I wanted to beat her ass for calling me weak or Chase ass for lying about how he really knew Brandon.

"What's your name?"

"Dutch."

"It was nice to meet you Ms. Dutch, but your services are no longer needed.

"Fuck you mean no longer needed, I'm that bitch, and you can't just come in here and take my livelihood away."

"Major!" I called my bodyguard to escort her out of the building.

"Now, who is Ms. Charmaine?" That's the main bitch I needed to let go; Duchess just so happen to run her dick suckers and let me know she been fucking my husband. Even though she will never fuck him again, I still didn't like the fact she was fucking his ass, and he was giving her all my fucking money.

"I'm Charmaine." This light skin, thick bitch with short blonde hair, stood up.

"It was nice doing business with you as well, but your services are no longer needed. Unlike Duchess, she may be able to come back but you my dear, I don't want to see you around here, you will never contact my man again, you will never contact my girls again. If I hear you have made contact with any of them, you and whichever girl that answered the phone for yo stupid ass will have a real fucking problem on y'all hands. No contact means no text, no call, no pop-ups, bitch don't even send a fucking smoke signal or we gone have a problem."

"Where's Chase? I put in too much work for his ass for you to come in and take over some shit that I helped him build." I stepped up closer to her filling the space that was once between us.

"Yes, and I'm that bitch that came in and took over what you claim you helped him build, so I thank you for making everything nice and cozy for me. Now, again your services are no longer fucking needed!" I spat. She tried to swing on me and I knocked her ass out.

"Major, come get her ass and show her to the door."

Major was my new personal bodyguard. He was so sexy and cock strong. Brown skin, low cut fade, pearly white teeth and big ass arms. He be anxious to throw niggas out at my discretion. He stood about 6'0 with a body made of steel. He grabbed her up and threw her over his shoulder. We all watched as he carried her out kicking and screaming.

"You will pay for this!" she screamed out when she finally came to right before he dumped her on her ass and slammed the warehouse doors.

"Is there anyone else who think they can play with me about my man? She got it easy, I was gonna beat her ass, but I decided to let her keep her pretty face. But, one slip up and that ass is mine. Any questions?"

The entire room was silent. Spinning around on my heels, I grabbed my Celine Drummed Calfskin Micro Luggage black bag and headed out the door.

Chapter 15

British

Tank and I had been lying in bed all day long just talking and trying to get to know each other more. I know y'all are saying, *shit it's too late for that you already pregnant*, but I still want to know the man behind the mask. So far, I have witnessed two different Tanks, and the one that was in the restaurant, I wasn't so pleased with.

Before I tell him about the baby, I want to see how he feels about kids, not just that though. Hell, I needed to find out how does he felt about having kids with me. The topic is sensitive for me because I have been pregnant before. The guy was crazy about me until the day I told him I was carrying his seed. That nigga threw me abortion money so damn fast.

I thought long and hard about going to buy me some new weave with that shit, but I didn't. Bringing a child into this world knowing his or her father didn't want to be apart from the beginning would be dumb of me. I wouldn't be able to fault anyone but myself if he never came around.

"What's on your mind?" Tank asked as he moved loose strings from my bun out of my face and placed a kiss on my forehead.

"Life."

"What about it?"

"Just trying to see where your head is with some things. As far as where do you see yourself in five years? Do you like to travel, what's your favorite food? What makes you tick? What makes you happy? I'm pregnant! What turns you on? What turns you off?"

"Wait... back up! You not just gone speed past that like you did not just announce that you were pregnant. Are you serious?"

"I'm double positive because I took two test." Tank jumped up on the bed and started jumping up and down like a little ass kid.

"We gotta go buy baby stuff, pick names, find a nanny, get you maternity clothes, and decorate the baby's room. Also, make a doctor's appointment today so we can see what we are having tomorrow, we gotta pick godparents, start a trust fund, build a tree house for my son and a pink playhouse for my daughter."

Tank mind must have started running a 1000 miles per minute. I was happy to see how enthusiastic he was about all of this. I thought his ass was going to flip out on me. He continuously jumped up and down on the bed, grabbed his phone, and called up Chase.

"Nigga we gotta celebrate, British is about to pop me twins out," he announced through the receiver. I don't know about that part, but we shall see.

***

I sat in the car while he loaded up all of the baby stuff he insisted on us buying. Telling him, it was bad luck to buy anything before six months was only going to make him furious. He had his heart set on buying out the store, and that's exactly what he did.

"You think you got enough?" I asked sarcastically.

"You think I didn't? I can always go back in!"

This damn truck is loaded down with shit and he talking about he can go back in. If he doesn't get his ass in this damn truck so we can go.

He got back in the car, and we headed right to the house. When we pulled up to the house, it was women just sitting on the porch.

"What the fuck do they want? I'm telling you Tank if any of these hoes about to come to me 'Woman to Woman' we are about to have a serious fucking problem!" I spat, as I sat up and crossed my arms.

"Girl calm yo ass down, those are my workers. I told all of them to come over to unload this damn truck and set the baby room up for you."

Walking on the porch, I watched as the girls all walked off and started unloading the truck. It was the beginning of July and if my boss would have called me to unload a damn truck that would have been the day my ass quit. I'm too pretty to sweat unless it's during sex. Then sweat could be dripping off his nose into my mouth, and I wouldn't give a damn.

***

Surprisingly, things have been great between Tank and I. Even after I blew that bitch's head off who obviously thought it was ok to give my man some head in our bathroom. I know he never asked me to be his woman, but shit, when you take it upon yourself to woman-nap a bitch for days and fuck her brains out, then that makes shit official in my book.

When I left out the house this morning, I couldn't help but to stop and admire the details of the baby room. The ladies did such a good job with the nursery. We will not know the sex for at least four more months, so we settled with green and yellow for the colors of the room. Tank stayed up all night putting together a crib. For some reason, he thinks it's twins, so he bought two. Deep down I know he will be an amazing father. He's been cooking me breakfast, rubbing my feet, my back, having someone to come over and give me a massage and a mani/pedi, and I am loving every bit of him spoiling me.

When I decided to move here, I literally left everything behind. My house is on the market, and I quit my job. I was ready to start brand new. Brenda, my mom, tried to talk me out of moving but that's only so I could stay and help her with her damn bills. Every month she pulls that, "Well I guess I gotta go to the church to get help with my light bill. You know they are about to cut me off." And my reply is always, "Well,

I would help but I don't want to intervene with the work of the Lord. He already has it worked out for you mama. Gotta go bye!" She is always with the shit for real.

"British Monroe... British Monroe!" the nurse called out so I could go to the back. Today is the day I find out how far along I am and get my first ultrasound. Tank should be walking through the door any minute; he said he wouldn't miss this for anything in the world.

"Hello British, I am Dr. Payne we have gotten all of the little things out of the way as far as blood work and another urine test. Now we are at the major part, the part I am sure you have been waiting on."

She started with a simple breasts exam and then felt around my stomach before she started with the ultrasound. Since I just missed one period, the vaginal ultrasound is the one she wanted to perform today—that would give me more of an accurate reading.

The doors burst open, and Tank rushed in once she started to insert the long vaginal stick inside of me. He was breathing heavy, and it scared me. From the look on my doctor's face, he scared her ass too.

"Shit baby, what's wrong? You just scared the hell out of me."

"I'm sorry B, I thought I missed everything and was trying to hurry up and get into the room before I missed anything else."

"Hey Dad, you are actually on time. Have a seat." She gestured for him to sit down and he didn't move, he just stood up beside me holding my hand.

"I'm ok, just go ahead," he replied, His heart was beating so fast I could feel it through his palms. You could tell he was excited as shit.

Moving the drum around a little, we started hearing a sound of a washing machine.

"You hear that? That's the heartbeat, and it's a strong one, might I add."

Looking into Tank's face and even though he was a big bad tough guy, at this moment, I actually saw his heart. He was smiling from ear to ear and kept kissing on the back of my hand. I turned to glance at the screen, and that is when I saw my babies on the screen. Yes, I said babies. It was two little munchkins in there. They were so tiny, and as of right now they both were just little dots in two separate sacs indicating that they will be fraternal twins.

He tried to turn his head away to wipe a tear before it fell, but I saw it. Seeing him emotional made my heart melt, and I could not wait to experience this journey with him.

"From the measurements of the babies, it looks like you are around four weeks and six days. Your due date will be expected around February, but it all depends on how the babies are growing if I will let you go all the way to 40 weeks or not. Until then, just take care of yourself and those babies. I will see you again next month."

"Thanks, Doc!" Tank replied as he helped me off the table and onto the floor.

We left out the building and headed home. Well I headed home I don't know where Tank ass went, he just said he would meet me back at this house later on. I decided to stop at the store and grab me a bottle of red wine. I know I read somewhere that I could have at least a glass a day.

***

I woke up that next morning to Tank feasting on me like I was a dessert and he had just eaten his main course. Something about the way he was eating me was different. Usually, our sex is rough and painful, but right now, it felt like he was making love to my pussy. Making him aware that I was awake, I began moaning. Realizing I was woke he slid up and stared me in my eyes. He didn't say a word, but he began tongue kissing me like his life depended on it. In the midst of our kiss, I felt him slide his dick inside me. Holding the sheets, I prepared myself for a wild ride, but it never came. His strokes were slow and meaningful. It's like he was giving me his love through each pump. It was so intense my juices were flowing down my legs. He continued to kiss me as he made love not just to my mind, but to my body as well. He was sliding in and out of me with so much passion before I knew it tears were pouring down my face. I was not crying because I was sad; I was crying because the shit was feeling so damn good.

I couldn't hold back any longer. "Baby, I'm cumming. Please don't stop."

Never speaking a word, I felt his dick swell up and right there in the morning sun, we came together.

"I love you," he whispered in my ear as he rolled over and wrapped his big arms around me.

Tank has proven himself to be a gentle giant and I love this feeling that he gives me. His presence alone, gives me butterflies, when he speaks to me, my heart melts, and when he makes love to me, I get lifted. He gives me a love high like no other, and my heart yearns for him. My body quivers at the thought of him coming home to me and all that sexiness. Hmmm hmmm hmmm, I love me some Tremaine "Tank" Williams.

"I love you too, baby," I whispered back and drifted off to sleep.

Chapter 16

Chase

"You know if she catches you calling me she gone fuck you up, right?" I said to Charm.

Cookie told me she told her specifically not to contact me anymore. Now I know Charm may not have seen what Cookie is capable of, but I have. I'm not scared for myself, shit I'm scared for her. She is really playing with fire.

"You could have taken control of her and told her you needed me. You know I'm a big damn part of this business, I know everything about you Chase, let's not forget that. You need to tell her to know her role, or I will teach both of you who the real head bitch in charge is."

"Charmaine, you already know how I give it up, and best believe my girl is the same way. I don't take kindly to threats against my lady or me. She let you go, and I'm rolling with her decision. She told yo ass not to call me no more, and you may want to listen. Cause when she comes for you, trust me, there is no stopping her."

After I told her that all I heard was the dial tone. I had to laugh on the inside because I know this was not going to end well for her. Charmaine is stubborn as shit and hate for anyone to try to check her and Cookie was gone be the one to do it too.

The shower water went off, and moments later Cookie came out in the best suit she could have ever gotten for her birthday— absolutely nothing! Since last week when we found out we were going to have a kid, it's like Cookie sex drive has turned to turbo. I'm not gone even front like waking up to head is a bad thing though. Her face is gorgeous and having a banging ass body is most definitely a plus.

At Monica's funeral, I told her I would never love a woman the way I loved her. Monica was my world and only after four years of marriage she was snatched away from me. She was leaving work late one day, rushing to get home in the storm. The last text I received from her said *"I'm coming as fast as I can baby. I have missed you so much."* When I replied back to her to tell her to drive safe and stop texting, it was too late. She never got a chance to read that message.

My wife was hit head-on by an 18-wheeler truck. He said he saw her swerve over into traffic, but it was too late for him to stop. The police report said the driver stated she must have been reaching down on the floor on the passenger side for something because at first, he didn't see anybody in the car, so he started blowing his horn. Then all of a sudden she jumped back up and turned her wheel hard to the left, but it was too late. She died instantly from the hard impact.

It took forever for me to even allow another woman to lay on her side of the bed. I bought brand new mattresses and donated all of her things to this battered woman's shelter here. For months I refused to speak to anyone. My brother Tank couldn't even get me to help him with our business. At that moment, I was just ready to let everything go since I had already lost my reason to live.

"Baaaaaby!" Cookie called out to me pulling me from my thoughts. She started crawling on all fours towards me. "Daddddddy!" coming up between my legs she eased her hand up the leg part of my boxers. She didn't have to go up that high since my dick was already hanging out the bottom.

Yea, I said that part correct. My dick is so big when I put it in her for the first time I swear I saw the head when she opened her mouth to scream my name.

Her hair was still wet from the shower she just took, so her curls were falling all over her face as she moved.

"I want to thank you for all that you have done for me. Since day one you have been there for me and showed me how I am supposed to be treated. Most men probably would have left that restaurant with me and fucked the shit out of me, but you, you just wanted to get to know London. The connection and attraction was there, but it was just the wrong time. Things for us have moved pretty fast. But, I always look at it as regardless of how fast we moved or how slow we moved, we would still get the same outcome if it were meant for us to be. I love you Chase, and I can't wait to rock that last name."

I moved her hair back and gave her a kiss on the lips.

"I love you more, baby! All I ask is that you know how to let me be the man in our relationship. I will never make a move without you; we will communicate about EVERYTHING, raise our kids to be great, and live life to the fullest. Now get up off the floor and lay down I have to go and meet up with Common to get some shit squared away. I will be back shortly to wax that ass."

"Wax that ass? Nigga, who says that shit," she joked.

"Bye Cookie, I will be back." I kissed her on the forehead and left out the house.

***

"Tell him no payment until the job gets completed. He never had a problem before so why the slip up now. If he talks and that shit gets pointed back to me then make sure you let him know he gone have to see me and it ain't for conversation. GET THE JOB DONE! He has 72 hours, nothing more nothing less," I spoke to my guy Common as he left out the building so that he could get the message back to one of my workers. I hate working with incompetent ass motherfuckers. If I give you a task and it's not completed how can you even think I am about to give yo ass any of my money.

"I figured you would be here," a voice came from the back of my building.

"Yo, who's in my shit?" I asked, pulling my gun from my waist and turning my infrared beam on.

"Your favorite girl!" Charm came from the back in this fishnet one-piece catsuit with the crotch out.

Running my hand over my face, I couldn't do anything but shake my head at her thirsty ass. She is begging for her life to end.

"For years I have lusted for you and never did I want to mix business with pleasure. But, since your new bitch decided to let the business part go, that only means it's more room for pleasure." She charged at me like a bull, jumped up, wrapped her legs around me and locked them at her ankles.

"Bitch, if you don't get the fuck off me." I started pushing her off me. The more I pushed, the harder she held her arms around my neck.

"I'm getting this dick today, and there is nothing you can do about it," she announced and licked the side of my face.

"So, this is the business you had to get squared away. Here I am thinking it was an actual nigga name Common and you really meant Charmaine. I came here because you left your phone at home and your mother said to call her because your sister Cassie just got her ass whooped by her baby daddy."

"London baby, it's not what you're thinking, let me explain!" I exclaimed.

"London? Like London Bridges falling down... falling down," Charmaine taunted her, causing Cookie to go into full beast mode.

Cookie threw my phone, and it hit Charmaine right in the head. She quickly jumped down and ran out through the back door and Cookie ran out behind her. By the time Charm was about to get into her car Cookie had snatched her ass back by her weave.

"I told yo ass if you contacted my man you would have to deal with me right. You should have asked someone if I was the bitch to test before you tried me. You see that fine man right there." Cookie turned her around to look at me while she had her in a chock hold. "That's my man right there and one thing for sure and two things for certain, I never play about my man."

"Well bitch, yo man is the one who told me to come here!" Charm yelled that lie out real quick.

"Baby, I swear she's lying, don't fall for that shit."

I felt like a real bitch begging her not to listen to Charmaine lying ass. Cookie threw her on the ground and stomped a mud hole in her damn face. Once she saw Charmaine wasn't putting up a fight anyway, she stopped.

"Fuck you, Chase!" She fixed her hair back in a bun and started walking back to her car.

"Cookie, please just stop and listen to me. This bitch was already here, see look she broke the lock to the back door." I pulled her back by her arm, and she started sending blows right to my face. When I let her go to start blocking them, she jumped into her car and sped off.

I ran back inside the building so I could grab my keys and my phone. After locking up the warehouse, I jumped in my car and sped off trying to find her.

***

I have been out looking for Cookie all night, she isn't answering my call, text and now I believe her black ass got me on 'Do Not Disturb'. It's entirely too early for us to be going through shit. There will be bitches and woman coming at me all the time, but she's gotta trust her man, know that they can't do shit for me and if they come with some bullshit, at least talk to me first before running off.

Calling British asking her where Cookie is would be like me talking to a brick wall. She ain't giving up no information; that's one lil' motherfucker who always goes by the G code, except when her ass snitched on Cookie about being pregnant. She told me Cookie popped her in the back of the head. I laughed so fucking hard at that shit.

Man, I miss my baby. She's got a nigga over here sick as fuck. I threw back shots of Patron, wishing I was deep in her guts right now.

RING RING

"Yea," I answered.

"What's good bruh, you heard from Cookie yet?" Tank asked.

"Nah, I'm setting up something tomorrow tho so be here. See if you can talk British into telling me where she is. This shit has got me bugging for real. When I see Charmaine's ass I'ma have to fuck her up myself."

"Gotcha bruh, this shit is fucked up. I'ma holla at B for you, though." We ended the call.

I grabbed my keys and took a ride through the city. I tried calling Cookie one more time, and still, my calls are going unanswered. I decided to head back home just in case she pops up. She is really starting to piss me off with this not answering bullshit.

"Fuck it, man; I'm about to go fuck with some twins tonight. I don't have time to sit around this bitch looking stupid." I went back to the house, laid across my bed, pulled my laptop out and went to Pornhub and typed in twins. I'ma get this nut out one way or another.

Chapter 17

Justin Blue

Cookie and I met years ago before she got married. I fucked up when I cheated on her with her friend Noelle. My mind was filled with regret since the day it happened. The day Chase called me to help with a cleanup job I was fucked up when I walked in the room. I saw Cookie's husband and her best friend, which is my old fuck buddy on the floor dead. I couldn't say anything to Chase because then he would know I knew them. I wanted to ask about Cookie, but I just kept all of my questions to myself not knowing what relation to them he was. That was until I made it to the hotel room and I saw her laid across the bed in tears.

Cookie and I were dating for about six months, and she had yet to give up the pussy. Me being the debonair man that I am, I thought I would ease in and out of those panties with no problem. Shit, she fooled my ass, the bad part is she would let me eat her pussy but wouldn't let me fuck. Talking about she didn't want any penetration. The bitch should have said that shit before I made love to that pussy with my tongue.

I have been telling Cookie for years that I would get her back by any means necessary. When Chase introduced us, she started stuttering like she was worried I would say something. I would never say the wrong thing and ruin my chance on being with her again.

Now that I know who she is with, the only thing I have to do is play my cards right, and she will be mine again.

"What's up my nigga, I haven't heard from you in a minute," I spoke to Chase through the receiver. I'm about to turn into a fucking damsel in distress on his ass. Nigga wanted me to help him now he gone have to help me... get his woman!

"Yea it's been a minute man, I am actually busy right now. Cookie has not been home, and I'm about to tear this city up looking for her ass."

Checkmate! I thought to myself.

"Say no more I'm on the next flight out. I am always down to help out with any situation, you feel me! I will call you when I land."

"Bet, good looking out, the more niggas I have, the faster I can get her back home." We disconnected the call. I packed a lil bag and headed to the airport.

***

"I need you niggas on a hunt for my wife and do not come back unless you have a fucking location. Do I make myself clear?" Chase yelled out to me and about 15 other niggas. I was cool with looking for her until he announced she was his wife. That shit will not fly with me. When I find her, she might as well consider that marriage null and void, cause Issa no for me son.

Everyone peeled out and headed in different directions, but I hung back a bit to kinda pick Chase's brain. She doesn't know too many people here so it's not too many places she can be besides a hotel. If I still know London how I think I do, then she will only lay her head at a Hilton.

"What's going on? I know she didn't just up and leave unless something happened."

"We got into this tiny argument, and it escalated quickly, once my old assistant blurted out that we had sex and still having sex, Cookie beat her ass like she stole something."

"Did you have sex?"

"Man, hell no. And if I did, I'm not doing it now so what does it even matter. Cookie's ass should have listened to me before she just up and ran the fuck off like that, especially when she is pregnant with my shorty. That shit ain't cool."

Nooooo, she can't be pregnant by this bitch ass nigga right here. I can't front, he runs shit in the streets, but he ain't good enough to be with London, PERIOD. With Brandon out of the picture, I am the only man for her and I won't let nothing or nobody come in the way of me getting what's rightfully mine.

"I'ma holla at you, I will start looking for her now. I will call you if I come up with anything."

We dabbed each other up and I headed to the nearest Hilton to start looking for her. Her car is so distinctive, so it should be easy to spot. She has a black Lexus Coupe with a pink MSU tag on the front with *I TEACH* on her back tag.

***

After searching the six Hiltons in Miami, I saw her pulling back into the Hilton Cabana on Collins Avenue. I started thinking of another plan to make this shit go smooth as possible. She got out the car in this tight ass body dress, fitting her body like a glove. Feeling my dick get hard, I started adjusting myself in my pants. Cookie always had that effect on me. Anytime a female just walks past you and make your dick damn near jump out yo boxers she's a bad bitch.

Looking at her, I had to come up with something quick. There's no way I was about to let him get to her. Thinking of something fast, I picked up my phone and called up Chase.

"I found Cookie, bruh. She was at the airport catching a flight back home. I tried to stop her, but she said she was not about to be played by another man."

"Aight bet, I'm headed to Columbus now then. I'm not letting her ass get away from me."

"Me either."

"Say what?" Chase questioned. I didn't mean to let that slip out.

"I was agreeing with you, bruh. Hello, hello." Chase's bitch ass hung up the phone. Fuck him; I had to make my move before she got too far away.

Getting out of my car, I jogged across the street into the parking garage. She was just about to get on the elevator. As the doors started to close, I stuck my foot in to make it open back up. Adjusting my shirt, I stepped in and stood beside her. The look on her face was priceless; she knew there was no way escaping me this time. I finally got her exactly where I wanted her— alone and in a hotel! I'm about to wear that pussy out and put her on a flight back home with me. If she knows what's good for her, she would not argue with me.

"Hello, London Bridges!"

"Justin, why are you here? I told you several times I did not want to be with your ass anymore. Once you fuck my friend, there is no more you and me."

"Apparently, you haven't heard! Your little boyfriend went back to that bitch he was fucking. He not out looking for you, he is too busy fucking a bad bitch." The doors of the elevator opened, and I grabbed her by the arm before she could get away from me.

We walked to her room, and I closely watched as she opened the doors to let us in.

"I finally got you all to myself. We are going to enjoy the moment and make love till the sunrise."

"I would really like that."

When she said that she had me puzzled as hell, but I'm glad she didn't put up a fight. Rubbing my hands together like Birdman, I walked up on her. I grabbed her by her ponytail, pulled her head back and gave her the wettest, sloppiest kiss ever. Surprisingly, she kissed back, I always knew she like pain. She looks like the rough freaky type.

"Can I at least shower first? I have been out all day. I know you don't want no pussy that's been sweating all day." Now she knows I want that pussy fresh and clean for daddy.

"Go ahead and get in the shower, I'll be waiting!" I laid back on the bed and started thinking about how I was about to tear that pussy up. After camping out at all these hotels, I started to get a little drowsy and drifted off to sleep before I knew it.

I've been waiting so long for this moment. Your body looks even better than I imagined. Those curves, those juicy ass perky breasts, and I can't forget about that freshly waxed sweet pussy. Come over here and let daddy make you feel better. She slowly walked over to me, pushed me back on the bed like she wanted to be in control. I could feel my dick swelling up as she unbuckled my pants. She came up and sat down on my face. I gasped for air when her ass cheeks covered my nose and my mouth.

"Hmmmm," she moaned, letting me know that she liked the way I was handling that pussy. Continuing to grind on my face, I gave her ass a squeeze and held her down tighter while I went crazy on that clit.

"Ohhhh shit Justin, I'm cumming, don't stop baby please don't stop!" she screamed out. Feeling her juices running down my face, I continued to suck on her clit making her go crazy and beg for me to stop.

"Wake that ass up!" a voice boomed out, waking me from my dream.

Chapter 18

Cookie

I have been hiding out for a few days now trying to get my mind together and make Chase sweat. In a way, I know since the short time Chase and I have been dating he hasn't fucked with her. I just wanted him to know how serious I was and for her not to fuck with me ever. She had gotten off easy. My intentions were to just blow her fucking head off, but I left my gun in the car. Of course, I didn't think I needed it since my man was supposed to be having a conversation with his guy Common.

To get my mind clear, I've been doing some shopping, and I went to my first doctor's appointment. I know he is going to be pissed because I went without him, so I will just tell him I didn't go yet. I just wanted to make sure everything was good, so when she mentioned an ultrasound, I declined. Hearing the heartbeat was enough for me.

Even though I have been away from Chase a few days, I still keep up with my girls. Duchess reached out to me yesterday and asked to have lunch with me. I know I didn't owe her ass an explanation, but since she came at me correctly, I told her the reason why I let her go. Thinking back to the moment I met up with her.

"I had to reach out to you to see what I did the other day to get fired. You just let me go after asking me my name, so yes, I was angry and puzzled as hell."

"No, sweetie. I let you go because you announced that you were sleeping with my ex-husband. Then you called me weak, so instead of beating your ass, I just decided to let you go. My issue was not with you; it was with Brandon. But, the fact that he did tell you he was married and you still fucked him, did bother me."

"I get that you were upset Cookie, but at the end of the day, this is my job. Neither Chase nor I made that man come blow money on me or anyone else. He did that shit on his own, FAITHFULLY. Now, I don't know what was wrong in your household, but it wasn't me. I was just after my paper. I have two kids getting ready to go off to college, and now I do not have a job. I invited you here for that reason. This job is needed for real. I'm not a burger flipping, milkshake making bitch. I'm a pop that pussy, suck a mean dick and I might lick an asshole if the price is right, type of hoe and I need my job back."

She really had me laughing my ass off at her ass for that shit. But, I respect her for coming at me, so I gave her the job back. Plus, the more she pop that pussy and licks assholes, the more money comes to me and mine. That damn Charmaine can never fix her lips to ask me for shit. And if I see that ass anywhere again, she better know I am fucking her up on sight.

KNOCK KNOCK

I opened the door to let British in. She's the only person who knew where I was, so she makes it her business to come up here daily.

"Hey boo!"

"Hey Cook, you know you got Chase ass going crazy trying to find you. He called me last night telling me everything. How he never fucked Charmaine, and how she only said that shit to make you mad. That was her way of getting rid of you. I believe his ass too, you need to stop being so damn stubborn and take your ass home."

"Girl, please! I will go when I'm tired of fucking myself and need that real shit in my life. As of now, I'm good on Chase. He should have tried hard to get that bitch off him. Shit, what I did to her should have been done before I even walked in. It would have made me feel a whole lot better to come in and see a bullet hole in her head than to see her ass straddled around my man. Plus, if he really wanted to find me all he had to do was turn my tracking device on from his end. The same one I gave the girls, I also keep one in my purse. When I need him, I will send a signal to his ass. He will come running," I stated. Shit, even though I know how to handle myself that won't stop a nigga from trying to snatch my ass up if they see me out in these streets alone.

"Well, it seems like you have it all figured out. I brought you dinner; I just forgot to get you a pop, so you will have to get that on your own."

"That's cool I had a taste for a sweet tea from McDonald's anyway so I will run out and get it. I will walk you out," I announced, as I grabbed my Celine bag and walked out the door with her.

***

Stepping into the elevator, I headed back up to my room. I scrolled through my Kindle app on my phone to see what I was going to read when I made it back to my room. I downloaded the series *No Way Out: Memoirs of a Hustla's Girl* by Latoya Nicole. British read it and told me it was based on the author's life. My ass can't wait till I can take a hot bath and relax on this soft ass bed.

"Hello London Bridges," a voice spoke, causing me to look up. Fuck! It was Justin. How in the hell did he find me and Chase's ass couldn't. This man is on some real Lifetime, 'I'm gonna get your sucka' bullshit.

"Justin, why are you here? I told you several times I did not want to be with your ass anymore. Once you fuck my friend, there is no more you and me."

He could not get that shit through his head. Making sure I would not run away from him; he had a good grip on my arm the entire ride up. The look of lust was all in his eyes so I already knew how I could get out of this. A little tease wasn't going to hurt; I was going to do whatever I had to do. Making my tracking device go off was the main thing. "Can I at least shower first? I have been out all day. I know you don't want no pussy that's been sweating all day."

He agreed on letting me go shower. His ass was so horny he didn't even realize I grabbed my purse and took it in the bathroom with me.

Turning on the shower water, I quickly locked the door, pulled my little tracker out, and squeezed it sending a silent signal to the main device at the house. Every tracker had a certain code for that girl so I already know Chase would be here in no time trying to rescue his babies.

Praying his ass didn't start getting suspicious, I started splashing the water around and singing "Dance For You" by Beyoncé, trying to make his ass believe he was about to get the business when I got out the shower. For a while, I heard him flipping the TV then loud snores started.

Not soon after that, I felt my phone vibrating.

BABY: OPEN THE DOOR!!

I eased out of the bathroom and let him in. It was Chase followed by Tank and Major rushing into the room.

"Wake that ass up!" Chase spoke putting his gun to the temple of Justin's head.

When he woke up and focused in on the faces, you saw nothing but fear in his eyes. Chase told me to go home so what he was about to do to him I had no clue, and at this point, I didn't even give a damn. I didn't have to tell Chase what was up when he saw Justin in the room; it wasn't any questions needed at that moment. That doesn't mean I won't have to explain how I know his ass later on. But as of now, I'ma let them handle their business and get my ass far away from this damn hotel.

***

Chase came home later that night with a pissed off look on his face. He undressed from the all black Nike sweat suit he had on earlier and jumped in the shower. I wanted so badly to jump in with him, but I knew right now wasn't the time to bother him.

20 minutes or so later, I heard the shower water go off. I hurried and sat up on the bed, Indian style. I already knew the questions were coming so I was mentally prepared for them by the time he came home.

He finished drying his body off, pulled the covers back, and got in the bed.

"Come rub my back. I had a long couple of days out looking for yo ass. Don't worry I don't have to ask you how you know Justin cause he told me everything before Tank took that nigga on a long ride. All of this could have been avoided if you had been honest with me from the first day I introduced you two. If you had told me the nigga was psycho, I would have never allowed that man to come here and help me look for you," he stated in a stern voice.

"I'm sorry, baby. I knew there would be nothing else between Justin and honestly, I did not think I would see him again. It was one of those don't ask don't tell type of situations. I never expected it to end up like this. I'm sorry, and it will never happen again." I kissed him on his back after rubbing him down and laid down next to him. He placed his hand on my stomach and pulled me closer to him.

"British told me she's having twins. I hope God can bless us with the same thing. I wouldn't mind having a little London and Chase Jr. running around here." He kissec' the back of my neck and fell asleep. The way he was snoring sounded like he was exhausted and was finally getting the best sleep he has had in days.

***

The next day

I headed to a quick meeting with my girls to see how things have been going with them. A few of the girls decided to quit so British, Tonya, Duchess, and I are going to the club tonight to recruit some new girls. This part is new to B and me, so we are going to peep Tonya out and see how she usually does this when the old bitch who used to be in charge is away.

"What's up, boss lady," Tonya spoke as she walked into the warehouse.

She had on this pleather short jumpsuit with some six-inch stilettos. I felt underdressed, I had on a skirt, but shit it didn't look anything like that. I thought I was supposed to carry myself professionally since I was coming in like a boss, I guess I was thinking of the wrong type of boss. I put on a pencil skirt and a cute little top to go with it.

Y'all know I am a schoolteacher, so if British and I weren't going to a restaurant for drinks, then I wasn't going anywhere. Clubs were never my thing in my profession. I refused to party with the kids I teach. Nevertheless, since my profession has changed, I guess my attire should too.

"Hey Tonya, you look all good and shit!"

"I know buuut what the hell you got on?"

Tonya is from South Carolina so she had this country accent and I had to laugh at the way she said it to me. I thought I looked pretty gah damn good. My skirt was tight as shit, making my ass sit out even more than is already does. The shirt I had on was low cut, so my breasts were damn near hanging the fuck out.

"Girl what you mean, I'm the boss, not the hoe!" She laughed, but then she thought about what I said, and that laugh quickly stopped.

"Boss man must didn't tell you, I don't fuck 'em, my mouthpiece is a motherfucker, and I can finesse the shit out of these niggas without even letting them smell the pussy. One thing you should know about me is, I'ma bad bitch and the fact that they can't have me makes me more desirable to them, and they go even harder to try to talk me into more than conversation. Conversation rules the nation and niggas wallets believe that. Now, if you don't mind, we're about to take you to the mall because you will NOT be walking with me looking like a fucking Stepford wife.

We all got into Chase's Hummer and headed to a boutique. They were dead ass serious about me getting out of this skirt and top. We walked into this store called Paris in Miami. Tonya walked me up to meet the owner. Her name was Paris, and she was this cute ass BBW. Her face was beat the fuck up, and I was dying to ask her ass how she gets those colors to blend on her eyes like that. Bitch had all the colors that are in a peacock feather on her eyelids, and that shit was fly as hell. She showed me around, but I wasn't impressed, so she took me to the back where she custom makes her pieces. She took my measurements and told me to come back in two hours, and she would have a dress made just for me.

Paris was plus size, but that didn't stop her from wearing her crop tops and high waist pants. She looked bad as hell I can't even lie. She was giving skinny hoes a run for their money. To be honest, her self-esteem was probably higher than mine was.

We left out of the boutique to grab a bite to eat. I enjoyed getting to know the girls. Even British was having a good time, and she never fucks with anyone but me.

"Bitch, didn't I tell you to stay away from my man." A car stopped in front of us, and a woman charged out right at Duchess.

I was taking back by the entire thing happening so fast, but once I saw it was more bitches getting out a raggedy ass Dodge Caravan that did not have the automatic sliding doors obviously. They were pulling hard as hell on that door trying to get it unstuck. I wanted to laugh but seeing them jump out of the van stopped me, so I had to throw my hair in a bun real quick. We were fighting in the streets like wild animals.

My dress was so tight when I dropped kick the midget one she went flying, and I thought my damn skirt was going with her. I was really going to be assed out, literally. British had to pull me off the midget and remind my ass I'm pregnant. Good thing it's no bigger than a bean or I probably would have hurt him or her or them. That lil' midget had it coming though. That bitch jumped out the back window and charged right at my knees.

When they heard the police coming, they jumped back in the van. The way it sounded you would have thought they were going fast as hell— the muffler was all fucked up! We laughed and continued walking up the strip. None of us looked fucked up, so we grabbed some food and walked back to Paris in Miami. I guess when a married man comes and spend money on you the wife has a real problem with that shit. I can't lie like I didn't want her ass to tap Duchess cause in a way, I still don't trust her.

Paris came from the back with my dress. The dress she had made for me was everything I could have asked for. It had a lil' hoe in it, but she still kept it a lil' classy for me. It was red and strapless with the back completely out, and it fit me like a lifestyle condom on a man with a big ass dick— tight as fuck! How she got that dress to stay up with no back and straps was beyond me, but this shit was cute as hell.

"Thank you, thank you, thank you! I couldn't have asked for a better dress. I hate wearing the same outfits from Rainbow and Forever 21's slut section. Sooo, you wanna be on my team? I need a badass designer like you, for my girls and me. They need original shit too.

"I would love too!" Paris blurted with so much excitement. "Of course, I would have to work around my shop hours, but other than that, I'm down for it."

"Here is my card, make sure you keep in touch." I threw her three stacks— one for the dress, one for the time she got it done in and one for her being a bad bitch. We headed back to Chase truck and did the dash back to the warehouse.

***

Pulling up to the club, I got out the car, and I swear it felt like I was the baddest bitch walking. Thanks to Paris for this bad ass outfit I was turning heads of niggas and nigga bitches, even the dikes were checking me out. I watched as Tonya peeped the scene before she would approach a girl. I don't know what the hell she said, but that bitch was smiling, and they went to the back. Duchess and I were waiting up front before she came back.

"I don't know where British is, but she should have been here by now," I said to Duchess while we sat and waited on Tonya to come back.

"Check out shorty right there, she is fine as hell," Duchess blurted, talking about the chick that just walked into the club. She was thick as hell, short curly hair, with a caramel macchiato skin tone, deep dimples, and a coke bottle frame; she was looking like a real snack. I decided to approach this one myself; I might as well step into boss mode.

I watched her as she took a seat at the bar, I heard her order my favorite drink, Amaretto Sour. I sat down beside her and ordered the same thing.

"I thought I was the only one obsessed with this drink," she said to me.

"Not at all, this is one of my favs."

"I'm Ashley, nice to meet you."

"I'm Cookie, so do you come here often?" I asked trying to spark up a conversation. I'm not sure how this shit is usually done, so I am just winging it for now.

"Yea most of the time, depending on if I had a bad day at work or not and needed to have several drinks. My job be taking me through it, I swear I have thought about crack a few times just to get my mind off the stress and headache."

"You should change jobs; no job should be that damn stressful. Here's my card, when you want a change just give me a call. I'm sure you will be a great asset to my team." I handed her my card, grabbed my drink, and walked back towards Duchess. I didn't have to say much; she hated her job and when someone says they have another one for you, the first thing you do come Monday morning is give them a call.

"That was quick, what you say to her?" Duchess questioned

"I gave her my card, she will call Monday."

POW! POW! POW!

Gunshots started going off in the club, and we couldn't get out of there fast enough. I had to leave my shit in the car cause they had security at the damn door. Here I am in my brand new ass dress under a fucking table, lying on a nasty ass floor on top of spilled beer and hot wing bones.

All of a sudden, my table was flipped over, and I was snatched up by my arm and pulled through the club. The person that grabbed me was shooting his way through the crowd. I swear it was like a scene in a Stephen Segal movie. I didn't know if I should be scared or happy that he was getting me out of the club. When we finally made it outside away from the crowd, we stopped running.

"Sorry for pulling you, but when I saw you get under the table I knew you were going to get trampled, so I pulled you up. I'm LaToya, but you can call me Toys."

She stood about 5'10, paper bag skin tone, and slim thick. Most slim chicks' ass ain't as big as hers tho. She got one of those big country asses, and you could tell that shit was homegrown. Dr. Miami had no parts in making that ass. Her bundles were at least 30 inches, those heels she had on made her legs look even longer and sexier. Now don't start saying Cookie ass is gay, cause I'm not, but Toys is fine though, and on a drunk night, she could get it.

"I'm Cookie. I thought I was getting rescued by a nigga. I didn't know a bitch had that much power to do that much shit, and yo ass got on six-inch heels. Bitch, you gotta teach me how to do that." We laughed and started walking towards my car. By then Tonya and Duchess were already standing there waiting.

"Glad to see y'all made it out safe, Duchess' ass left me as soon as she heard the shots. I'm glad I just recruited a new girl cause she's about to lose her job for leaving my ass under a table. But thanks to Toys, she got my ass up out of there real quick."

"Boss lady yo ass stay forgetting you pregnant, huh?" Tonya stated, honestly hell yea. I'm not used to all this baby shit yet. I never have morning sickness, the only things that lets me know I'm pregnant are these juicy ass breasts and my appetite.

Duchess started looking at Toys with the side eye. I wanted to tell her that she is not the one to fuck with from what I just saw, but I'ma let her find that shit out on her own.

"I gotta get home, thanks for the help tonight. I could use a bad bitch like you on my team too."

I passed her my card, and I headed towards the warehouse so the girls can get back to their cars. I gotta call up B to see what happened to her ass tonight.

Chapter 19

Tank

"See you later babe. I'm heading out with Cookie." British gave me a kiss and walked out the door.

Today was one of the worst days of my life. My mental had been fucked up, and I was having flashback after flashback. I popped two sleeping pills and a muscle relaxer to get my mind right. I didn't want British to leave, but I didn't want her to stay either. When I get into this mood, I have blackouts and wake up to bloody knuckles and holes in my walls, my car in some bushes, or a body lying in front of me. It was always a horrible scene when I finally snapped out of it.

This person I had become was literally taking over my life. Normal seemed farfetched; my life was too fucked up to be anything but normal again. In a way, I wish it was me being dragged off with my life had ending instead of having to live here and deal with this shit day to day.

I completely cut my psychiatrist off. British still does not know I suffer with this illness; I'm left with dealing with this on my own. Chase comes by and checks on me every now and then, especially when he knows it's been a few days since he has heard from me. He's good with keeping me out of bullshit.

If he finds out about me doing this lil' side gig for this man, he will flip the fuck out. He knows it would only mess my mind up even more. That's why he got me dealing with the girls only. Killing someone for me was like waking up in the morning and brushing my teeth; it was my new daily routine. I had no remorse for shit anymore. My mind started to sleep, and my body started to get heavy. I laid back on the bed and drifted off to sleep.

The sound of leaves being crumbled by someone foot was heard throughout the camp. We knew it was a group of them but didn't know how many, but we came prepared. I signaled for my friend to go across the street quickly and hide. The plan was to ambush them once they came passed us. Watching as he started camouflaging himself, I continued to lay low and held my position. We have not had any sleep in 48 hours so lying on this ground using these leaves as a pillow made me feel so comfortable, a little too comfortable actually.

BOOM! BOOM!

I was awakened from sleep I didn't even know I was in. If my sergeant had caught me, that would have been my ass. Men were running around everywhere shooting, and carrying people to a safe place if they had been wounded. When I looked up, I saw Horace being dragged away on the back of a truck. It was so much going on around me that I had to protect me. It took everything in me to keep lying low and keep shooting as many of them I could get before they all ran off.

That night when we made it back to our bunks, I started thinking about my friend and how much trouble he could be in. Sargent Troop walked in and started talking about the ambush and how they just received a tape. He popped it in, and it was two men from the ambush standing next to someone on their knees, with a bag on their head.

"We asked you to leave our country alone. We have one of yours, but that still will not stop us until we have the same amount of people taken from you as we had taken from us," one of the men spoke.

He removed the black bag from his head, and there was Horace proudly sitting like he was ready to die. Showing no weakness, he held his head high, and they cut the bitch right off.

I could feel myself fighting in my sleep, beating the hell out the man that took my friend. Continuing to stomp him, his screams only made me stomp him even more. I grew restless and tried to wake myself up, but I could not snap out of the dream I was having. I could see his body lying on the ground with blood everywhere. Rage came all over me as I replayed Horace's head getting cut off. I wanted him dead too, and I was not going to stop until he was gone.

"Taaaank... Taaankk... babe pllleasse stoooop!!!" a weak voice cried out to me, awakening me from my dream.

When I came to, all I saw was British on the ground with blood everywhere. She was crying silent tears because she could no longer speak since so much blood was coming out of her mouth, her head was busted, she was bleeding really bad.

"Fuuuuuccck!!! Baby, I'm sorry. I'm sorry. I'm sorry. I'm sorry. I'm sorry," I continuously said as I pulled her limp body into my chest and cried.

"What have I done?" I yelled out to myself. I was so fucked up I didn't hear her come back into the house. She has to be ok; I have to be able to tell her I'm sorry and this was an accident. I love me some British and the last thing I wanted to do was hurt her or my babies. "FUCK... MY BABIES!!!" Getting off the ground in a hurry, I called 911 and then called Chase. He always knows what to do in this situation.

After a while, I heard the door bust open, and it was Chase standing there in shock at the sight before him. Blood was all over me from holding her in my arms like a baby and rocking her back and forth. I kept whispering in her ear, "It's gone be ok, I'm sorry, It won't happen again. I will kill myself before I allow myself to hurt you again." I kissed her on the forehead and laid her back on the floor.

Running through the bushes behind my house, I waited until the ambulance and police left out of my house before I went back in.

Chase already knew the deal. This happened before, but that time the girl didn't make it. He had to tell the police he came over to check on things because I was out of town and he found her in the house dead with one gunshot wound to the head. I paid for all of her funeral expenses and gave her family 100K. I knew that would not bring their daughter back or make me feel better about killing her, but hey it was a start.

Once they left out of my house, my first thought was to go and kill myself. I couldn't do that yet though because I needed to check on B and the kids.

Walking back in the house, made me relive that moment all over again. Shaking my head back and forth to focus, I ran into the bathroom, showered and changed before I headed to the hospital.

***

"How is she?" I asked the doctor right when he walked in the room.

"She's a fighter. I can tell you that Ms. Monroe came in here pretty badly beaten. She has fractured ribs, and her collarbone was broken from the force of, what I'm thinking were continuous kicks in one spot. Surgery went well; we had to put a few screws in her shoulder. She will need some physical therapy, but other than that, she will be okay. Just give her a while to recover.

"What about the babies?' I was almost scared of his reply.

"I'm sorry, but the babies didn't make it. They were too small and going through that much trauma put a lot on them." He gave me a sympathetic pat on the shoulder and walked out of the room.

Walking over to her bed, I watched as she slept. I rubbed her head, sat down beside her, and laid my head on her thigh.

"I'm sorry B, I promise you I never meant for this to happen. I should have told you about my problems then you would not be here barely holding on. I killed my kids, and that's going to haunt me for the rest of my life. I don't deserve to live anymore. This PTSD is getting the best of me, and I will not allow it to make me hurt any more people. This is my goodbye." Kissing her on the back of her hand, I stood up and walked towards the door.

"No!" I heard her whisper causing me to stop and turn around." Don't do it; we can get through this together."

She slowly eased her eyes open, and they were bloodshot red. Tears started to roll down my face just looking at all of the pain I have caused her. "I know you didn't mean to do this. I could tell by the look in your eyes that it wasn't you. You were talking and fighting in your sleep, and I tried to wake you up, that was my mistake. I forgot my phone, so I turned around. When I saw you there, it scared me, and I wanted you to wake up out of that dream you were having. You had tears coming out of your eyes, so I knew it was a horrible dream."

She started to cough, and blood came up. I gave her some water and rubbed her head.

"Until I get myself together I can't be with you, British. Seeing you like this is killing me and I'll be damned if I allow it to happen again."

"You're not leaving me; we are going to get through this Tank. We've both just suffered a big loss, losing you too would make me go crazy. Please stay!" She reached for my hand. I sat down in the chair next to her bed and watch her fall back to sleep.

Chapter 20

Chase

"I don't know what bum off the streets you hired to get this job done, but it looks like I have to do it myself."

I had Common hook me up with this private hitman. So private that I didn't know him and he didn't know me. We just spoke through money. When he completed the job, he got his money, and that's how that went. He has been working for me a while now, and I damn near want to set up a meeting with him to see what the fuck is going on in his head. You never leave a job half done, this time he only left the man paralyzed on one side. He did a half job, so he half got paid, fuck that.

I never wanted to get my hands dirty, my father had enemies everywhere, and he made sure even in death, that they still paid for whatever they did to him. His old ass didn't tell me what they did, he just told me they had to go, and I'm making sure of that. 250 down 50 more to go then I'm shutting this shit down and just focusing on the girls.

Cookie is starting to get the hang of things. When that shit popped off with British and Tank, she was at the club recruiting more girls. Calling to tell her that news was hard as hell. I probably was wrong for telling them that I just found her like this, but I didn't want my brother to get in trouble for some shit he couldn't control.

Another situation that couldn't be controlled is what happened with Charmaine and Cookie. Charmaine told that damn lie so fast, and Cookie ass believed it even faster. She made my girl run off on me, so I had to find a way to fuck her, knock-kneed penguin toed ass up.

"Hey babe, are you ready to go to the hospital?" Cookie asked in a taut tone. I could hear the nervousness in her voice.

I told her how bad things were and she had been holding off going to see her. She already told me she was going to kick Tank big ass when she saw him, so I already told his ass not to be at the hospital when she got there. Granted British is ok and understands what happened was a mistake, but Cookie doesn't get that shit.

We got into her car and headed to Merci Hospital. She reached over and grabbed my hand as I pulled into a parking spot.

"Chase I'm telling you, if my cousin is damn near about to die, you're about to lose a brother. I swear to God." She started hitting her fist against her other hand. "I want him to suffer."

"Babe, calm that shit down for real. Go up here and see your cousin, she ain't on that bullshit with him, so it's not your place to do or say a damn thing to him. Now, if I'm gone have a problem with you up here, then we might as well not even get out. I've been real fucking nice to you and let you have your way, but I'm still the fucking man in this relationship. Yea you caught two bodies, but that shit doesn't mean nothing to me. Like I said British is fine. Get yo ass up those stairs and check on your cousin and leave that bullshit in this fucking car." Cookie had been getting away with a lot of shit, starting with her ass running off and then lying about Justin's bitch ass.

Just because I love her and she's pregnant with my shorty doesn't mean I can't put her ass back in her place. She runs shit with those girls, but that hardcore attitude does not need to make it in my fucking house. She needs to go back to being that soft ass Cookie, the Cookie whose pussy gets wet at the sound of my voice. That's the Cookie I need to be seeing right now.

We made it to her door and Cookie hesitated before knocking. This girl started crying as soon as she looked at British and ran over to her. I just shook my head. She cried so hard it made British start crying.

152

"Hey B, how are you feeling today?" I asked as I walked over to her bed.

She looks a lot better than she did. Tank really did a number on her. I always tell his ass he needs to stay on those meds. It's been a long road for him, but with all of our help and much prayer as my grandma would say, he will get out of this and get back to the Tank he used to be.

"I'm ok, just a little sore but nothing I can't handle. Your brother has been here taking care of me. He barely let a nurse do anything because he wanted to do it all. He changes my bandage, helps me to the bathroom, washes me up while I'm in the shower, and get this, the nigga even wipes my pussy for me after I piss." She made all of us laugh with that one.

"He should do all that since he is the reason why you're here," Cookie mumbled.

"Cookie, I know you're mad at me, and I promise this was not done on purpose." Tank emerged from the corner he was sitting in.

It was so dark over there we didn't notice him when we came in. "I was completely out of it. British knows I would never do anything to hurt her or my kids. I'm fucked up about this too, that's my girl right there in pain, and those were our kids that are gone now. You're right I should wait on her beck and call since I am the one who got her here and I have been doing that. She is good with me. Now I can't tell you to accept it because that's your cousin and you don't want to see her hurt. Like I told her, I would take my own life before I do this to her again." Cookie just nodded her head and turned back to British who was now sleeping.

"We are going to leave y'all alone and let her get some rest." I headed out of the door first, and then Cookie followed. "Tank... take care of my cousin!" she announced, sticking her head back in the room. I reached for her hand, and we headed back to the car.

***

After leaving the hospital yesterday, I realized I needed a break from all of this. One of my girls were in the Dominican Republic and called to tell us how beautiful it was, so Cookie and I packed our bag and booked a flight out the next day. I realized I never got the chance to really date her since everything moved pretty fast for us. I'm not complaining or anything just saying it moved quickly. But now here we are, I'm on the balcony of our suite, looking at this beautiful view and watching an even better beauty walk around and get dressed.

"Which one should I wear baby, this bikini swimsuit or this one." She stood there completely naked with all of her sexiness showing. My dick started to rock up before I could even answer.

"I don't know, come here and let me get a closer look." She walked over to me still looking at the bathing suits, so I scooped her up and tossed her on the bed.

"Chase stop, you know we gotta go down and meet Candy." That's what her mouth was saying, but the juices between her legs said otherwise.

Coming up between her legs I gave her a kiss on her lips before I made my way down to her other set of lips. I could tell she was holding her breath with anticipation because she let out a moan just by me getting close to her pussy. She opened her legs up wide, and I went right for her clit, massaging it softly with my tongue. I could feel her legs starting to shake, and her back started to arch.

"Shit baby..."

"You like that?" I started eating that pussy like it was a medium well steak with potatoes on the side. Before I knew it, she screamed out.

"I'm about to cummmm, baby please don't stooop... shiiiiiit!!!"

Her pussy started gushing as soon as she said that. I kept my tongue right there and made sure I cleaned her up. Nothing touched the sheets; my mouth was the only thing she needed. She rolled over with the look on her face like she was waiting on me to drop off some dick too.

I got up and answered her question.

"The bikini, I wanna see you in the bikini."

She threw the pillow at me so fast, got up, and went into the bathroom to get dressed. That girl is crazy she was just rushing me to go downstairs to meet Candy, now she's mad cause I won't dick her down like I just licked her up.

Chapter 21

British

It was rough waking up in the hospital, and it only hurt worse when I found out I lost our twins. At first, I wanted to kill Tank ass and make him really feel my pain. That night I walked back in the house, he scared me because he was talking to himself and swinging at the air like he was fighting someone. Once I saw tears coming out of his eyes, I decided to wake him up. If I had known I was going to get the snot beat out of me, then I would have let his ass sleep that shit off.

The more he punched and stomped me, the more I screamed out for him to stop. His eyes were open, and it looked like he was out for blood. If I didn't manage to muster up that last cry before blood started filling up in my mouth, then he probably would have beat me to death.

I started to black out, but I could still hear everything that was going on around me. Hearing how scared he was confirmed that he didn't know what he was doing. He kept repeating he was sorry over and over again. I tried to speak, but no words came out, only blood. Knowing that he has PTSD makes me want to love on him even harder. He did a job for his country, and now he is suffering behind it.

"Good morning, Ms. Monroe. I have your medication here to drop off at the pharmacy and your discharged papers. We have an appointment set up for you on Monday to meet with your physical therapist. We want to get some strength back in that arm for you." The discharge nurse gave Tank my papers and helped me into the wheelchair.

He picked me up and put me in the front seat of his truck. I hate being dependent on people, although I love all the attention I am getting.

"I cleaned the house up and everything that I bought for the babies I put it in the basement."

"Tank, I know you are just trying to help, but I really do not feel like talking right now. I am in a lot of pain, and I really just want to get home as soon as possible."

"Ok baby, you hungry?"

"Now you know I'm hungry, that nasty ass hospital food was the worse I have ever tasted in my life. It's almost as worse as Cookie trying to make noodles."

We went to the drive-thru at McDonald's, and I ordered me chicken bacon ranch salad and a sweet tea. I refused to go into a restaurant looking like I've been hit with the ugly stick.

***

I watched as Tank went into his bag where he keeps his clippers and pulls out several bottles of medicine. One pill at a time he made sure he swallowed them. That made me feel good because I ain't seen this nigga pop a pill since I have been here.

To you, I may be crazy as hell for staying with this mentally disturbed man who just beat the living daylights out of me, but I am sure we have all done something crazy in our lifetime, mine just so happen to be staying with after a man put his hands on me. All I keep telling myself is that he will get better with my help. So I know I can't leave him. That's what he is used to, people saying they love him and leaving when they find out this nigga does not have the sense that God gave him.

"Good morning, baby. I'm glad you finally woke up, I made you breakfast, I have a massage therapist coming in a little later to rub some of that soreness out of you," Tank spoke as he laid down in the bed next to me. "I'm really sorry for not telling you about my problem. I just didn't want you to run away like the other people have. I can be too much to handle sometimes. Not that I'm calling you weak and saying you can't do it, but I know how I can get sometimes," he softly spoke as he rubbed my head that was laying on his chest.

"Tank, it's ok and trust me I'm not like them. I would have stayed with you regardless of what you told me. I fell in love with you, and it would be hard as hell for me to fall out of love with you just over something like that. The good thing is my father suffered from PTSD from when he was in the military. I watched my mother take care of him, granted it was hard, but she did it. She didn't give up on him, and I will never give up on you. I love you Tank."

"I love you more, B!"

Chapter 22

Charmaine August

"Yes Office Warren, a prostitution ring! They have drugs in that warehouse, and I'm almost certain that if you turn the lights off and do one of those black lights like they do on *First 48*, then you would see blood all over those floors."

"And how would you know all of this?" he questioned.

"An old worker of his told me all of this, and I just know it's true because she has never lied to me before. She even said when she went there the other day she got jumped by the boss and his bitch, I mean his woman."

"Ok, ma'am we will check this out for you."

"I don't need you to check it out. I need you to do your fucking job. Arrest them. They are pushing drugs out of that warehouse; I just know they are. I know those poor girls they have working for them are being held against their will and they barely give those poor girls money. If you run their names in the database, they are probably runaways." I was trying to make my story as believable as possible, I wanted Chase and that damn crumbled up Cookie bitch to feel me. If this shit doesn't work, trust me, I have a plan B and C.

"Ok, let me get to it!" He hung up the phone before I got a chance to add that he may be over there raping those poor girls too.

I'm sure you guys already heard about me. I am Charmaine August from New Orleans. I'm standing about 5'4 ½; I like to add the half so I can seem taller. I'm what they consider high yellow complication, freckles on my face, short blonde hair, and my ass is fatter than a swamp possum with the mumps. I moved to Miami right out of high school, having only a few dollars to my name. Working dead-end jobs here and there until I ran across these chicks coming into my job before they went into work. I couldn't help to think about how it all happened.

"Welcome to Burger King, may I take your order?" I asked the ladies approaching the register.

"Yea, gimme a second. Do y'all sell fruit here cause I know when I get through shaking my ass tonight I'ma go home with some high roller and he gone wanna eat this pussy till I pass out. I need this shit to taste like a fucking fruit salad." They both slap their hands together and let out a loud laugh.

"No, we only have burgers and fries, ma'am."

"I thought the sign said I could have it my way, so I'ma need y'all asses to get me some fruit for this pussssssyyyyy... bow bow bow!!" They started twerking like they were not in front of a kid getting ready to order him a kid's meal. Deep down I wanted to laugh at these country ass women, but all I could do was shake my damn head.

"You look like you tired of flipping burgers and dropping those soggy ass fries, come holla at us when you wanna make some real money."

They left out of the restaurant, and I slid the card in my pocket that she gave me with her info on it. Once I met up with the girls, they told me what their jobs were. They worked at a strip club called "Shake Sum". I'm sure whoever came up with that name felt like saying shake something was too proper for a strip club.

I met the head nigga in charge, and after my first couple of tries during amateur night, he hired me. The first time I had to perform a dance solo I couldn't think of shit, so my ass learned the entire dance from Players Club, Diamond did the damn thang. My music started playing, and I did my sexy walk on stage.

"Temperatures rising, and your body's yearning foooor me..."

R. Kelly and a few shots of tequila had a bitch in the mood. My eyes locked with this fine ass man sitting in the front with three other men. Looking like bags of money, finessing them would be too easy. I gave the most attention to the one in the middle. After my set you already know he called me over to his VIP section and it was on from there. The guy in the middle was Chase and Tank was right next to him.

I became one of many girls he had working for him. Once I got tired of fucking like crazy, I went to him and asked for another position. I needed to be the head bitch in charge. By becoming his assistant, I went to different states making sure everything was straight with the girls and collect the money.

Liking my job isn't even the half of it, I loved my job. The money was easy, and I didn't have to do half of the shit the other girls had to do. Although my ass wishes I could have fucked the shit of Chase before his bitch let me go, in due time everything they have will fall, and I will reap all of the benefits of it.

"What's up D, what's the plan?"

"They've got some new girls coming in now. I found one of them, and she's down with the plan that I presented to her. We gotta take them down. I do not like that bitch Cookie, or her cousin British. Them bitches are not about to just come in and take over our shit like that," D announced.

"If this shit does not go well with me calling the police then we gotta make another move and quickly."

"Bet, I'm out before anyone see me talking to yo ass." She got out the car and ran back over to hers. I probably shouldn't put in that much effort to get back at them, but that bitch took everything from me, including my man.

Chapter 23

Chase

"Ok, Thanks for letting me know," I said as I clicked the phone after talking to my uncle.

He works for the police department, and it seems as if someone is trying to say I got some other shit going on. Other shit like sex trafficking, prostitution, drugs and a list of other shit. He didn't give me the name, but I'm almost certain I can figure out who it is.

The lights from the tracker for one of my girls started going off. Looking at the screen I could see it was Lexi, so I grabbed my bag and left out the house.

Me: Cookie, I gotta make a run real quick. Lex needs help.

I jumped in my Lamborghini and did the dash to the location of the tracker. I'm glad she was in the city, so I didn't have far to drive.

Pulling up to this abandoned house, after looking at the location as I drove past, I came back around the corner but parked a block and a half away. I grabbed my pistols and walked through some trees to make my way to the side of the house without being seen.

As I looked through the window, I see two guys one standing up beating his dick looking like he getting ready to buss all on Lex's face, and the other one was taking his pants down. She was tied up with no clothes on. I'm glad we put the tracker on the girl's wrist so it would be easy for them just to press right there and send a signal.

Once I saw he was about to start raping her, I sent a bullet through the back of his head, right through the window. His body fell to the ground, and the other guy stopped beating his meat and started looking for his pistol. I had already peeped it was by the side door where his pants were, so I wasn't worried about him making it there before I fucked him up. He turned to run to the door but quickly fell to the ground once I sent a bullet through his ankle.

Rushing into the house, I started to untie Lexi. I gave her the gun and watched as she got up off the ground and walked over to him. He was crying like a bitch, but just like me, Lexi didn't give a fuck. She emptied the clip on his ass. She grabbed her clothes and started putting them back on as we left back out the house.

"Boss man, I was so happy to see you. I met these fraud ass niggas at the club, and he swore up and down he had so much money and lived in this fat ass house. I should have known something wasn't right when we got into his Cutlass!" Lexi spat, making my ass laugh. She knows I always find the niggas for my girls. I only hook them up with the best, and I never find a nigga in the club. So that was her mistake.

"Since when we start letting y'all find people to fuck with on y'all on? What if they killed yo ass soon as you got inside that raggedy ass Cutlass. Everything I do, I do it for a reason, not so I can be in control. Next time yo ass will listen to me, or it won't be a next time. You follow?"

"Understood!" I dropped her back off at the house with Patrice and headed to the warehouse. It was something I needed to handle.

"Meet me at the warehouse!" I clicked the phone and headed right to the warehouse. When I pulled in, she was already there waiting on me.

"Glad you could come, it was something I needed to talk to you about. An officer called me today and was telling me about an anonymous tip he got about my warehouse. Saying how I'm picking up runaways, sex trafficking, prostitution and shit like that. Which you and I both know is not going on. One thing stuck out to me though, when he mentioned me selling drugs out of my warehouse. Now, stop me if I start getting things wrong, which I highly doubt. But, you are the only person I had that conversation with, and you are the one who presented it to me. Asking if I could meet your cousin because he is this big time dope boy, and I could gain a lot from fucking with him. Right or wrong?" I questioned Duchess.

"Right, but boss..."

"Stop! Now, how did all of this get back to the officer? He even mentioned your cousin's name saying he was told I was working with Hulk now. All of this can't be a coincidence. I already know you are about to start lying your ass off and saying everything but the truth, so I will save your breath for you.

"One thing you bitches will never do is try to cross my fiancé and I" Cookie stated announcing herself as she came front the back with her gun pointed at Duchess. "I let you come back in after you gave me some sob ass story about how your kids needed money for college and all that bullshit, but FUCK THEM KIDS." She shot her once, right through the ear, and blew her brains out.

"Thanks for meeting me here, I was hoping you read the text I sent on the way to help Lexi's crazy ass out."

"Yea, how did that go?" she questioned.

"Her ass got caught up with the wrong niggas."

"They're asses gone listen when I tell them to sit the fuck down and let you handle that part. Oh well, I already called the cleanup crew. Let's get back to the house; I need some dick." She jumped in my Hummer and sped off. I'ma have to hide those keys, that's all her lil ass want to get in lately.

Chapter 24

Tank

It's been a few days since British has been out of the hospital. I've been playing Jeffery Butler for her ass. I gave her a bell to use when she needed something, and you better believe she used it every chance she got. It didn't bother me though. I needed to do whatever I had to do to get her back to 100%, including pay for a therapist to come to our home instead of her having to go to the facility. She still has a busted vein or whatever. The doctor said in was in her eyes, so they are both red. It will take a little while before those heal completely.

When I was at the hospital with B, I learned that Valentin didn't die from those bullets through the neck. Now, I have to find him and finish the job. I know British is probably thinking I'm out fucking off because when my phone ring I go outside to take the call. If she finds out what I do, she just might leave my ass. I leave out the house when my phone ring so I can get my next job assignment.

This nigga hit me up every other day with someone new to knock off. The sad part is one of the niggas I had to kill was my uncle, my mom's brother. When I got his name and the amount they wanted for his head, shiiid, that man was no longer my uncle. Uncle Charles who? Nah, Ion him! That was my reaction when I saw I was getting 900K for his head, that nigga was dead before nightfall.

"Ay B, I gotta make a quick run, so I will be back. Call or text me if you need anything."

"Tank, it's one o'clock in the morning, what could you possibly have to do this late? Cookie already checked on the girls, and Chase is at home with her in bed. So, who is she?" She sat up in the bed and folded her arms."

"Who is she? British, I know you are not asking me that like I'm about to go out and fuck a bitch. You are the only bitch I'm fucking, and since you have been hurting, my hands have been the next best thing—oh, and this pocket pussy that I purchased. Other than that, ain't no bitch been on this dick, believe that."

Not waiting on her response, I walked outside to my shed and grabbed the tools I needed to finish this assignment. I grabbed my guns and headed towards my truck. As I walked past the front porch, British ass is now standing there holding a strip of Magnums in her hand.

"Before you leave make sure you take these with you cause if you think you're about to go fuck a bitch or some bitches unprotected then come back and fuck me you got another thing coming witcho crazy ass."

This bitch barely can see out her eyes but managed to find some condoms I had in my dresser.

"B, you better take yo ass in the house, for real! This ain't the time to come fuck with me. Now I got some shit to handle. You need to go lay yo ass back down."

I jumped in my truck and sped off. I watched as she ran back in the house. British's goofy ass was the least of my concerns.

As I made my way to Valentin's home, I noticed a car making every move I made. They would wait a few seconds, but as soon as I switched lanes, they were doing it shortly after. I sped up through traffic trying to shake them. Whoever it is I will have to deal with them later.

Pulling up to Valentin house, I parked a block away and climbed the tree adjacent to his home. I grabbed the binoculars I got from Horace before they cleaned his bunk out, and surveyed the area. It was three guards out front and two on the roof. Once I get past them, the rest would be easy.

I pulled my Barrett M98B from around my back, counted to ten and started dropped bodies like draws. I was so far away they didn't know where to start shooting. Once the first five were down, I waited until the rest came out with guns drawn. Eight people ran out, and all eight were fucked up as soon as they walked out the door or came from behind the house.

After waiting ten more minutes to make sure everyone came out and left him in alone, I climbed down from the tree. Still being cautious, I kept my pistol out and put my Barrett around my shoulders. My military senses were kicking in and every little sound I heard I pointed my gun in that direction.

Maid to the left- *POW,* Butler coming out of the kitchen downstairs *POW!* Today no one lives.

I walked some more and was almost at his room door. Pushing my way in, I scanned the area carefully but saw no one but him laying in the bed. I slowing made my way to his bedside and pointed my gun at his head. He was sleeping peacefully then all of a sudden everything started to be a blur to me.

Fuck! I thought to myself. I tried to close my eyes and shake my head back and forth to stop my PSTD from kicking in at this moment, but I couldn't shake it.

The sound of leaves being crumbled by someone foot was heard throughout the camp. We knew it was a group of them but didn't know how many but we came prepared. I signaled for my friend to go across the street quickly and hide. The plan was to ambush them once they came passed us. Watching as he started camouflaging himself, I continued to lay low and hold my position.

The sound of a gun clicking pulled me from the exact dream I always have. Valentin was laying there shaking with a gun pointed at me. So much was racing through my head, but I was so in shock, I forgot to pull my gun back up and point it at him.

"I knew you would come back to finish the job. You killed all my damn security; I couldn't let you get me too. It's good thing you left one good side, so now I can finish what you started. Fuck you and your boss."

He raised the gun up some more, and I just stood there frozen. *POW! POW!*

Chapter 25

British

Three months later

I sat on my patio watching the sunset trying to think of something to get Tank out of this funk he has been in. His birthday is a few days away; he turns 31. I thought about taking him on a cruise, but his ass talking about he watched the *Titanic*. So, a cruise was definitely out of the question.

I'm not sure what I'm doing, but I needed to start planning. He did everything he could do for me to get back to my old self and even paid for a few surgeries here and there to enhance my beauty. Like these nice perky 38Cs I'm rocking, and this extra flat ass stomach. It's only right that I show my appreciation back.

I'm glad I followed him that night his ass ran off, or I would be real fucked up right now. I thought I was about to lose him when I walked into the room and saw him standing there stuck with a gun being pointed at him. I got chills up my spine just sitting here thinking about that shit.

Three months earlier

Tank got another thing coming if he thought I'm about to sit here while he go to fuck a bitch. I don't give a fuck how much pain I'm in; I'm about to follow his ass and fuck the both of them up. He put me through too much shit in so little time to allow him to just creep off.

Once he drove off, I ran into the house and grabbed the keys to his Maserati. I knew he couldn't get away from my ass in this. Every move he made I was right on it. At first, I thought he noticed me because he started speeding up, so I fell back a little bit.

He pulled up to this big ass house and parked a block away, so I parked two blocks away. Once I saw his ass climbing in that tree like Tarzan, I knew this wasn't a bitch house. The car made too much Vroom Vroom noise for me to drive off without him seeing me, so I decided to stay and make sure he was good. I grabbed one of his guns from under the seat and started walking towards where he parked his car.

POW! POW!

Several rounds were going off, and I quickly ducked behind a tree. After a while, he climbed down and made his way across the street, and I followed. I don't know what my ass was thinking knowing damn well I don't know what I'm doing, but for my man, I will move a mountain.

Stepping into the gates all I saw was bodies everywhere. It had to be at least ten plus bodies laid out on the lawn. Making my way to the front door, I heard two more shots go off then I saw what looked like a maid fall over the banister, and a butler fall as soon as he stepped out the kitchen. My baby was fucking up everybody; I made a mental note to suck his dick properly when we make it home.

He stepped into this bedroom, so I quickly but quietly I made my way up the stairs. It was no noise for a while then I started to hear someone speak, but it wasn't Tank.

"I knew you would come back to finish the job. You killed all my damn security; I couldn't let you get me too. It's good thing you left one good side, so now I can finish what you started. Fuck you and your boss."

When I saw how that man was barely able to hold his gun up and Tank was just standing there in a daze, I knew something wasn't right. He had this big ass gun around his shoulders and held a pistol in his hand. He could easily fuck this man up, but he was stuck. The old man raised his gun up towards Tank.

POW! POW!

I shot him once in the chest and once in the throat.

Tank finally snapped out of that daze and turned his gun towards the door at me.

"Baby wait... it's me!" I yelled out before he started to shoot.

"British, what are you doing here?" he questioned as he grabbed me by the arm and pulled me down the stairs.

"Well, you're welcome! Apparently, I was here saving your life."

"Get your ass back home, and I will meet you there in a minute."

When I made it back home, I took a quick shower and laid on the bed pretending to be asleep. He came in the house on ten ready to let me have it. As soon as he sat down on the bed and started taking his pants and shit off, I came around and started kissing on his neck.

"Baby, I'm sorry," I said, kissing him between every word. "I thought you were going to fuck a bitch, so I followed you." I was now sitting on his lap in a straddle position. "When I saw you dropping bodies, it turned me on. I don't want to argue; I just wanna fuck."

He tried to pretend like he was still mad at me and didn't want to kiss me back until I moved off him and pulled out his meter long 'King Kong' dick and started sucking it like this nigga just won the Little Lotto, and I wanted 75%.

"British," Tank blurted, snapping me out of my thoughts.

"What's up, babe?"

"Why are you not dressed yet? We got 20 minutes to make it to the doctor and yo ass sitting over there in la la land."

Shit, talking to y'all ass got me in trouble. Did I forget to mention I was two months pregnant? Once I fully healed, Tank and I were fucking like jackrabbits. He wanted to make sure I got my babies back, and sure enough, my ass is popped again.

This is my second appointment and Cookie has an appointment too. She actually finds out what she is having today. I'm so excited her for and Chase.

***

"British Monroe!" the nurse called out indicating it was time for me to go to the back. This is my first ultrasound, and I'm nervous and hell.

175

Tank helped me up on the bed, and we waited on the nurse to come in. He reached over and grabbed my hand and gave it a gentle squeeze once he heard the doors open up.

"Good morning mom and dad, are you guys excited?"

"Yes, ma'am!"

She started squeezing the warm gel over my stomach and moving the little tool thingy around. At first, we heard the strong heartbeat then the images started to appear on the screen.

"I hope you guys have enough room because you will have not one but two little additions to the family."

I was so in shocked I couldn't say anything. To be expecting twins again the second time around is truly amazing. If Tank ass does anything to hurt these babies this go round, that nigga is gone have to die for real.

"Thank you so much, and yes we have more than enough room for them." He kissed me on the forehead and helped me get off the table.

"I have a surprise for you," Tank stated as he stepped in on the driver side of the car.

"Really! Give it to me." I closed my eyes really tight and held both of my hands out.

After a few minutes of him still driving and me still holding my hands out, I opened one eye and looked at him. "Yo ass could have said it wasn't in the car, got me sitting here with my hand out and shit."

"Brit, you acting like I told yo ass to hold your hand out. All I said was I had a surprise for you."

"Asshole." We road about 20 more minutes before the truck finally started to slow down.

Pulling up to the front gates, my mouth instantly hit the floor. The gates were made out of two lions on each side with the design of the gate meeting in the middle where it forms the letter W. As we drove up the spiraling driveway, I easily fell in love with the acres of immaculately kept landscaping. I was so in awe with the different sculptures cut into the bushes until my eyes finally landed on a mansion that looked as if you could fit our house inside of it five times or more. He came around and opened my door for me.

"Tank, Oh my fucking gawd!!!" I spoke with so much excitement, looking up at the house.

"Now you can close your eyes and hold your hands out." I closed my eyes really, really, tight and held my hands out and felt him sit something inside of my hands.

"Open them!"

Opening my eyes, it was a box, and he was down on one knee.

"Open it, British!" My heart dropped into my stomach. I opened the box slowly and it was a damn key.

"British Lynne Monroe, will you move in with me, again?" I started to chunk this box at his head, here I am thinking he was about to ask me to marry him.

"Yea... sure," I said in a dry tone, closing the box.

It was beautiful white daffodils and purple bellflowers in the front of the yard. Walking up the steps, I noticed a cute white swing on the porch and the wooden sign above the door that said, *Welcome*.

Pushing the door in, I stepped into the foyer and was met with roses everywhere and two older ladies holding a sign that said, *TURN AROUND*. Once I turned back around, Tank was back on one knee, but this time he has this massive ass ring out.

"British, since the moment I met you and the four beautiful days we spent together. Whether it was willingly or unwillingly, we enjoyed the time spent together. When I got you back to the house, and you didn't kill me, that let me know then that you were meant for me. I didn't expect to live another day, but you only made love to me like nothing even happened. I have taken you through hell and back, and you still stayed with me, pushing me to change my ways and helping me get better. I'm glad you didn't give up on me, I'm glad you didn't give up on

177

us. All I need to know and I would like to know in a hurry because my knee is starting to hurt, will you marry me and make me the happiest man on earth."

"Tank baby, yes I will marry you." I ran to him and jumped into is arms. He put me down and placed the fattest rock I have ever seen on my finger.

"Congratulations, cousin," Cookie said as she came from out of the kitchen with a piece of chicken in her hand.

"Thaaanks boo. Look at this damn ring girl, shiiiiitt!" I was so excited I forgot to look at the rest of the house. I can't believe I am about to be Mrs. Tremaine "Tank" Williams.

The road has been rough for us, but so far, we have been pushing through it all. I talked him into going back to his therapist. He needed to see why he keeps having those damn dreams, and I will be damned if I wake up dead.

Chapter 26

Cookie

RING RING

"Hello."

"Hey BG, it's Daddy!"

"Hey, Daddy, I'm glad you called. I was intending on calling to check on mom. How is she doing?"

"That's why I called; she's not doing good. I took her to the doctor yesterday, and they only gave her a few days to live. The cancer has spread throughout her body and is now causing her organs to shut down. She won't eat anything and if she does it comes right back up. You need to get here as soon as possible baby girl and tell your mother goodbye."

At this time tears were rolling down my face, but I did not want my dad to know. I needed to be strong for him. My mom and I have not always been close. That's why it was so easy for me to just up and leave, even though I already knew she was sick. My mom has been in and out of my life when I was growing up. My dad was a hustler, so he was rarely home. British's mom, Auntie Sin— my dad's sister— raised me. Dad and I have always had this close relationship even though he was hardly home. Regardless of what time he got in he always came over and got me dressed for school and dropped me off. When I got old enough to drive myself, I woke up one morning to a spanking brand new 2010 Mustang. It had just come out, and I was the proud owner of it.

"I will be there as soon as I can get a flight out, Daddy. Tell her to hold on for me."

"Ok BG, I love you."

"Love you too, Daddy."

My dad has been calling me BG for years. I think just saying baby girl is way cuter. I got out of bed and started looking for clothes I could still fit. I'm five months pregnant, and I am big ass a house, literally! When Chase and I went to the doctor, we found out that we were having identical twin boys. Chase had the names picked out before we even left the doctor's office. Chase Jr. and Chance were their names.

I was happy he got his boys that he has been praying so hard for.

"Wake up, baby," I said to Chase while pushing him back and forth. That only made his snores grow louder.

I rolled him on his back, slid my big ass under the covers, pulled his dick out and started sucking it like a blow pop, going from the tip of his dick to putting wet soft kisses on the bottom of his balls.

"Hmmmm…"

I felt him adjusting his body so I could take it all in, and I did just that. Putting his dick all the way in my mouth, I didn't stop until I gagged and his dick was covered in slobber. Slurping it up, I continued to bob up and down on his dick until I felt him getting ready to explode.

"Baby, don't stop, I'm about to cum."

I stopped sucking his dick and climbed on top of him. Even though I'm already pregnant, it's just something about his nut shooting inside of me and feeling this dick start to thump like a heartbeat as he emptied his seeds off in me. Once he finished coming, I was in the perfect position to start riding him. He always goes bananas and tries to push me off cause his dick is extra sensitive, but I keep riding him until I cum. Since I have been pregnant, it doesn't take much for me to nut anymore.

"Now, that's how I want you to wake me up every morning," he blurted out, causing me to laugh as I attempted to lay down on his chest, but my belly was in the way.

"Get up shorty; you got nut running all down my side."

"Nigga, that's yo nut too."

"Naw, my shit skeets up, yours run down," he stated. I grabbed my pillow and started hitting his ass with it.

"You're stupid baby, but I love you." I leaned in to give him a kiss before I headed to the shower.

"Who was that on the phone?"

"My dad, my mom is dying," I said in a nonchalant tone.

"What the fuck? And you say that shit like it doesn't faze you, Cookie."

"It does bother me Chase, but I have to push it to the back of my mind and stay strong for my daddy. On top of that, I never show emotions in front of people."

"I'm not people; I'm your fiancé. If you can wake up with your hair all over your head cause your bonnet slipped off in the middle of the night, and I still fuck the shit out of you in the morning, then you can cry in front of me."

"Chase you can't even compare the two. Shut up! Besides she's not dead yet. She will be ok till I get there."

"I know you guys relationship wasn't perfect Cookie, but at the end of the day, she is still your mother. I will call up my guy so he can fly you right there so hurry up and wash that pussy." I turned to get into the shower to wash all of his nut and sweat off me.

As I stood there putting soap on my towel, I started to think about how much Chase was right. You only get one mother, and I am about to lose mine. My mother hasn't told me she loved me in over four years. I haven't felt a hug or a simple kiss on the cheek in forever. It's crazy because these are things I've always yearned for and I was never giving. I can't lose her before I get the chance to tell her how much I love her and that I forgive her for not being there for me. I've held on to this grudge long enough, and now it's time for me to make amends with the past.

"Cookie baby, get up." The sound of Chase's voice pulled me out of the trance I was in.

Looking around, I see that I was sitting on the shower floor with tears streaming out of my eyes. I never knew how hurt I was because I have always held my resentment towards my mother inside of me. I hated her for not being a mother to me. I didn't get that talk about my period from my mother, that came from my auntie, talks about sex and how you should wait till marriage came from my dad, and hell truth be told, by the time he told me he was about a year too late. I had already popped this pussy for a real nigga two or three times.

He reached down to help me out the shower and dried me off.

"If you want me to go with you for support I will. You don't have to do this alone."

"No, baby! Go ahead and get ready for your meeting, I will be ok!"

Walking into my closet, I started putting clothes in my overnight bag so Chase could drop me off at the airstrip.

***

My dad called me as soon as I landed telling me to hurry up and get to the hospital. I called British's sister Alicia to pick me up. Traffic was so backed up, a drive that would usually take 20 minutes turned into an hour.

Finally, we pulled up to the hospital, and I got out running as fast as these babies would allow.

"Excuse me can you tell me what room..."

"Cookie, come this way!" my cousin Alicia yelled out.

We went running down the hall to the elevator. Once I stepped off the elevator, I could see my granny and my Auntie Evie on the floor crying. I was stuck and too scared to move. Seeing their reaction I could tell I was already too late. Walking over to a seat by the elevator, I sat down and just cried my heart out. I felt so bad for not being here for her.

"Cookie, baby, come and tell your mother goodbye."

My daddy reached his hand out and walked me to the room. I was mentally trying to prepare myself for just seeing her lifeless body there. All I wanted to do was kiss her on the forehead and tell her I loved her.

He pushed the door open, and my mom turned her head towards me. Running over to her bedside, I couldn't do anything but scream and cry because I thought she was already gone.

"Oh God, Mommy I thought I had lost you before I got the chance to say goodbye."

"Your father told me you were on the way and I had to make sure I held on just a little while longer so I could talk to my baby girl one last time," she spoke in a soft and shallow tone. "London, sweetheart, I'm sorry for not being there for you like I should have been. I should have been more of a mother to you and did things mothers and daughters are supposed to do. I was so caught up in being free and living my life that I forgot about the life that I brought into this world. Your father and I both made mistakes, but I don't want you to ever doubt our love for you." She stopped talking to take a deep breath and started rubbing me on my hand.

Looking down, she noticed my stomach and tears started to fall from her eyes.

"You are going to be a better mother than I was. Don't make the same mistakes I made, Cookie. You be there for your child as if your life depended on it. Oh, and tell Chase I said thank you for the flowers, they were beautiful." I looked around the room and saw she had a room full of flowers.

"Mommy, did Chase send you all of these flowers?" I got up to read the card on some of them.

"Yes, baby. A little while ago, the flower shop up the road delivered them. I thought they would never stop coming." She smiled and started watching me as I read the cards.

Card 1: *They say give your loved ones their flowers while they are living, so I wanted to shower you with lots of flowers to show you how much we care about you.*

Card 2: *I promise to take care of your daughter for the rest of our lives.*

Card 3: *Even if Cookie can't say it right now because she is probably crying, she really loves you*

Card 4: *Even though I have never met you, I bet you are just as beautiful as the daughter you created.*

I could not believe Chase went out of his way to do this. That man definitely knows how to make me feel like the luckiest woman on this planet. As I got to the last card, I turned around to talk to mama.

"Hey Ma, did you get a chance... Ma ... Ma!" I sat on the bed next to her and continued trying to wake her up. "Mama, please get up. Please, I didn't get the chance to say I love you yet."

The doctors started coming into the room. One nurse checked her pulse, and then I heard her take her last breath. Then the monitor started to make the noise when a person has flatlined.

"3:16 p.m.," the other nurse called out for the time of death of my mother.

"NOOOOOO!!!! MA, NOOOOO!!!" I dropping down to my knees.

"It's gone be ok baby girl. We have to let her go." My dad had tears in his eyes, but he wouldn't allow them to fall.

"I will give you a moment alone." The doctor stepped out of the room, and I climbed in the bed with my mama as my daddy stood and held her hand.

Chapter 27

British

Tank has really been going through it today. Watching him as he throws glasses and vases against the wall pumped nothing but fear into my heart. I wanted to pull him into my arms and just hold him until the pain went away. He was so frustrated I was afraid to touch him thinking he would snap out on me.

"Tank, baby, please calm down!" I yelled out to him, but it seems like everything was going into one ear and out of the other one. He continued to pace the floor back and forth.

Walking into the bathroom, I went and pulled out his medicine that keeps his head on straight and a glass of water. I watched as he swallowed each pill individually. Then start to explain what was going through his mind.

What he said I didn't expect, but I knew one day it would come to this point. Hearing that he wanted to kill his boss sent chills through my spine because I didn't know what the outcome would be. He has been working for this man a while now and has never met him. People that high up has crazy power and who knows what this man is capable of. You have to go through someone just to get a message to him. So I'm sure this task won't be easy for Tank.

"If you go, I'm going with you," I manage to muster up. I was worried about what he would say, but just like the last time when he froze up, I came through and saved his life. I don't want him to freeze up again without me being there to help him.

"British, you know you don't have to come right. I don't want anything to happen to you or my babies. If something happened, I would kill myself."

"I know baby, but I promise to be careful, and I will stay in the car."

"No! It's not a good idea. Just stay here, and I will call you when I leave and call you once the job is done. Deal?"

"Deal!" I said that but I didn't mean that shit at all. Once he leaves out, I will be right behind his ass, just like the last time.

"Don't be mad at me baby, come here."

He pulled me in closer to him and gave me a kiss so wet it made my damn knees weak. He slipped one hand into my panties, and the other one was rubbing my stomach. He knows how to make this pussy wet as hell. Since I have been pregnant, it doesn't take much at all. Just a slip of the finger and a bitch pussy is leaking.

"Hmmm…" he massaged my clit with one of his fingers, damn near making me nut all over his hand.

"Take those off!" he demanded, pointing down at my panties. I snatched those panties off so fast that I damn near lost my balance.

Lying back on the bed, I watched as he got undressed and stared at my pussy while he stroked his dick.

I laid there just waiting cause I knew he was about to give me the business. He went in head first like he always does, inserting his tongue inside of my pussy, moving it forcefully in and out. Then he did something that he has never done. He turned me over and started eating the booty. Laaaaawd… I damn near lost my fucking mind. No one told me how good that shit felt. He was going crazy licking and sucking and licking some more. Good Lord, sweet baby Jesus just lay me at the throne.

"Tank, shit baby, I'm about to cum." That only made him eat it up more. I felt like the nigga was trying to do a 'Mortal Kombat' move and take my soul.

He slid his arm under my stomach and propped me up all the way in doggy style position. I just love when his ass gets cock strong with me in the bedroom. He pushed my back down making me arch it more so he could get deep up in it.

After about 15 more minutes, he finally exploded on my ass, then fell on top of me.

I watched as he took a shower and got dressed. I was hoping his ass didn't take all the car keys to make sure my ass stayed put. When he walked out the door, I hurried up, cleaned myself off, grabbed a set of keys, and waited until he pulled off before I hit the alarm.

***

Waiting outside of this warehouse, I watched as he got out of the car and swiftly made his way inside. It's just something about when he does these jobs that turn me the fuck on. Tank is the type that as soon as he walks into the room his presence alone demands attention.

That night when he walked up to me at the bar and started talking, my pussy instantly started purring. I was happy when Cookie left with Chase because I didn't want to be the only hoe leaving with a man I just met. He had not asked me to leave by the time Cookie left, but I knew it was coming. I was looking too damn good for him not to even entertain the idea of taking my ass home.

He must have knocked a damn hole in my wall that night from the headboard knocking against it so damn much.

RING RING

The phone going off pulled me from my thought.

"Hey, bitch."

"Girl, why are you whispering?" Cookie asked as she whispered too.

"Cause bitch I don't want Tank to hear me. Why is yo ass whispering?"

"Bitch… cause you're whispering… the fuck." She made me bust out laughing at her stupid ass.

"My ass is supposed to be at the house, but I'm out here watching Tank."

"What he doing?"

"Girl… this nigga is about to interrupt this meeting and kill his fucking boss."

"Boss? Who? I didn't know he did anything else besides help Chase with the girls."

"Yea he is something like a bad ass hit man, and this shit's got me turned on."

"It's just the babies, that's all," Cookie replied.

"How long have you been there?"

"Not long, I think he said the meeting starts at eight o'clock, but the guy usually comes early."

"Where's Chase?"

"Girl, his ass is gone to a meeting too. He just left not too long ago, saying he likes to be there before his crew arrives so he always goes in early."

"Wait B, where did you say this meeting was?" she questioned.

"At a warehouse, why?" I replied with much hesitation.

"You don't think it's the sa…"

"Fuck... Cookie, I gotta go, bye" I clicked the phone and ran inside the warehouse.

Chapter 28

Tank

"Tank, baby, please calm down!" British yelled out to me as I threw another glass vase against the wall.

I am trying so fucking hard not to lose it. Trying to get past everything with my friend, I realized killing is what's causing me to keep having the dreams. I reached out to the guy who hooked me up with my boss for my assignments, and he refuses to let me just walk away.

I can't stop until I finish out the contracts he already paid me for. I guess it was supposed to motivate me to finish them faster, so he paid me two mil up front. At the time, I was just happy about the money. Having shorties on the way, I was trying to make sure my family was straight, so I took the money. A few weeks after is when I realized hearing gunshots made me reflect back on being in the military.

"B, I gotta get out of this shit one way or another." I took a seat on the bed, and she came over with a glass of water and my pills so that I could calm down.

"Take this and just lay back, babe."

"I'm sorry for making this mess; I will make sure I clean it up before I leave out tonight."

"It's ok, baby. I would rather it be a glass vase hitting the walls than me." She started to laugh, but I wasn't in the mood for jokes.

"That's true baby, and I promised not to ever put my hands on you again. I will forever keep my word on that."

"You said you had somewhere to go tonight?"

"Yes," I replied.

"Where?"

"I'm going to kill my boss!"

I got off the bed and walked away because I knew she was about to come with the bullshit. The truth is, this is something I won't be able to walk away from. Until this man is dead, he will forever have this hold on me.

"Tank!" Shit… here it comes, I know she gonna try to talk me out of it.

"If you go, I'm going with you!"

I turned to look at her and was in complete shock at what she just said. She has been telling me I needed to give it all up and just pay my boss back, but shit, I don't give money back. That shit is considered pain and suffering money, and I earned that shit.

"British, you know you don't have to come right. I don't want nothing to happen to you or my babies. If something happened, I would kill myself."

"I know baby, but I promise to be careful, and I will stay in the car."

"No! It's not a good idea. Just stay here, and I will call you when I leave and call you once the job is done. Deal?"

"Deal!" She rolled her eyes so hard at me. I know she means well, but I just can't take the chance of something else happening to her or my babies.

"Don't be mad at me baby, come here." She walked over to me with her lip poking out.

Pulling her closer to me, I grabbed her face and gave her the wettest, sloppiest kiss ever.

"I love you B, and I will die if anything ever happened to you." I reached down, rubbing her stomach with one hand and her pussy with the other one. I needed to make her feel good before I just up and left her here worrying about me.

"Hmmm…" She let out a moan as she bit her bottom lip. Her pussy was wet as hell, and I couldn't wait to put my face all in it.

"Take those off!" I motioned for her to take her panties off and lay back on the bed.

When she took her panties down and opened up her legs, I saw that pretty pussy drooling. Her pussy was just sitting there screaming 'come eat me', and I did just that. I feasted on her until my mouth got tired. I didn't care how many times she yelled out she was about to cum; I was trying to take her soul.

Flipping her over I did just as Jhene Aiko said, I ate dah Booty like groceries. That made both of us lose our mind. She was moaning out cause it was feeling good and I was praying her ass didn't poot in my face.

I saw that pussy was dripping wet so I had to get inside of them guts. I slid one hand under her stomach and pulled her up into doggy style position. I eased my dick inside of her because I knew it was tight as hell, but once I worked my way in, I went into beast mode. All you heard was her ass smacking again my pelvic bone. Every time I pulled back some, she would tighten up her pussy lips and damn near make me buss.

"Shit, Tank! Slow down, baby!" I heard what she was saying, but I couldn't pull myself out. Her pussy was the softest place on earth, and I wanted to sleep in.

I wrapped my arms around her waist like I was giving her a bear hug from the back and started murdering that pussy, ramming every inch of my dick inside of her. I started to feel myself about to cum, so I pulled it out and released all over her ass.

"Damn baby that shit was good!" I moaned out as I fell on top of her.

"If you don't get yo heavy ass off me, I know sum!" she spat back at me.

"My bad baby, the pussy got daddy knees weak." I laid there for a few minutes before I got up and took a shower. I needed to get my mind right before I left the house.

***

My guy told me they have their weekly meeting at this warehouse and my boss man is always the first to arrive—until tonight that is. I will already be inside waiting on his ass. We have never met before, but if this nigga thinks that he can just have a hold on my life like this, he has another thing coming. After I get rid of him, I'm laying my guns down for good.

I made my way inside the building. It was at least another hour before boss man is expected to come in, so I laid low and held my position until I heard the opening of a door. I stood up, guns drawn and without hesitation, started firing. I didn't want to wait until he had a chance to pull a gun out on me, I emptied the clip on him, then pulled out my other gun to finish him off.

POW! POW! POW! POW! POW! POW!

I walked over to him so I can send another one through his head, to make sure his ass was dead. The closer I got, the more my heart started to race like I was about to have another episode.

"Baaaabbbbby… no, no, no, no, no... fuuuuuuuck!" I screamed out as I pulled British off the ground. British baby, please get up… get up… get up… get up. I shook her over and over again before I pulled her into my chest. "B, I'm sorry. I did not know it was you. Why did you come here, B? Baby whhhyyy??" I screamed out with tears pouring out of my eyes. I could not believe what I just did. "You have to get up British, you hear me? Baby, I need you to get up, please get up… please get up!" I continued to yell out, but she never did respond. I was just sitting here holding her with blood pouring out everywhere.

"I told you I wasn't living without you, B." I turned the gun on myself, put my finger on the trigger and stopped as soon as I heard someone come into the door; I pulled my gun back quickly and pointed it at the door.

"What the fuck? Tank what the fuck did you do bruh?" Chase yelled out as he ran over to B trying to help me get her up.

"Bruh, I didn't know it was her, I swear!" I quickly replied.

"What the hell are y'all even doing here, Tank?" he screamed out in a panic while pulling out his phone to call the ambulance.

"I came here to kill." I paused for a second and thought about it. "Wait…What the fuck are you doing here?"

TO BE CONTINUED

Made in the USA
Lexington, KY
06 September 2019